To Christina and Tracie

# Tree Tall
## and the
# Horse Race

**Shirlee Evans**
**Illustrated by James Ponter**

**HERALD PRESS**
**Scottdale, Pennsylvania**
**Kitchener, Ontario**
**1986**

**Library of Congress Cataloging-in-Publication Data**

Evans, Shirlee, 1931-
  Tree tall and the horse race.

  Summary: Tree Tall, an Indian boy living on an
Oregon reservation in the mid-nineteenth century, wins
a horse of his own in a race but finds his victory
marred by misunderstanding and prejudice. Sequel to
"Tree Tall and the Whiteskins."
  1. Indians of North America—Juvenile fiction.
[1. Indians of North America—Fiction.  2. Racing—
Fiction.  3. Christian life—Fiction.  4. Oregon—
Fiction]  I. Ponter, James J., ill.  II. Title.
PZ7.E8925Tp  1986      [Fic]      86-7659
  ISBN 0-8361-3414-1 (pbk.)

TREE TALL AND THE HORSE RACE
Copyright © 1986 by Herald Press, Scottdale, Pa.  15683
  Released simultaneously in Canada by Herald Press,
  Kitchener, Ont. N2G 4M5. All rights reserved.
Library of Congress Catalog Card Number: 86-7659
International Standard Book Number: 0-8361-3414-1
Printed in the United States of America
Design by Alice Shetler

91  90  89  88  87  86  10  9  8  7  6  5  4  3  2  1

# Contents

1. A New Beginning — 9
2. Big Dreams — 23
3. Getting Ready — 35
4. Threat of the Stallion — 49
5. Plot of the Soldiers — 61
6. Get Ready—Get Set . . . — 74
7. And They're Off! — 85
8. His Head High — 98
9. Condemned — 111
10. Thunder Hawk — 122

*The Author*—135

# Tree Tall
# and the
# Horse Race

# 1

# A New Beginning

THE BROADAX came down with a whack on the iron wedge, splitting the cedar log from one end to the other. Tree Tall grinned as he put the ax down. He looked at his father. "Much faster with tools of the whiteskins."

Gray Seal stood with his forked pole tucked under one arm, keeping his weight off his crippled leg. Although he now wore the white man's clothes, Tree Tall understood the heart of the man. It was a proud Indian heart. One that had all but been crushed with defeat after the white man's rifle had found its mark and injured Gray Seal's leg two long rains ago.

"The Indian boy makes fast work of the cedar boards," his father remarked, still not willing to give more credit than necessary to the ways of the whites.

9

It was good working with his father—good helping to build a new lodge for their family. Tree Tall just wished it did not have to be here— on reservation land where they had been herded like the white man's cattle. Gray Seal and Tree Tall's mother, Little Pine, had approved his idea of building their lodge in the small clearing rather than in the center of the large Indian encampment by the river. The soldier captain had also approved.

"The only bad thing," Tree Tall had remarked to his father, "it is so far for the women to carry water from the river." It never once came to his mind to help, since Indian men never carried water.

"Little Pine and your grandmother have a water carrier now, since you brought us the girl Bright Sky."

The boy's thoughts went back to the time he had found the Indian girl. "It was strange, finding Bright Sky to be the daughter of your friend who died," he commented. "I, too, thought she was of an enemy tribe when I found her on my way to Oregon City to look for the white boy Jerome. Bright Sky is small for seeing ten times of the long rains."

His father nodded, looking closely at his son. "You are now thirteen times of the long rains. If we were in our old village, and Gray Seal's leg had not been hurt by the whiteskin's rifle, he

10

would be hunting and making the canoe now. Would have many things put aside to give as gifts at a festival during the time of the long rains. Tree Tall would soon go off alone to seek his own guardian spirit." Gray Seal's wide face drew down in sadness. "Our old ways will never again be the same. Gray Seal cannot hold a rainy-time festival now to hear his son name his guardian spirit and give gifts to our people. Now white soldiers make themselves guardians of all Indians."

"Maybe soon we will have enough of the white man's things to give as gifts, after Gray Seal and Little Pine make more trades with the white store-man. But Tree Tall already has his guardian Spirit—has had it long before we left our old village."

Gray Seal was staring at his son.

"It is Jesus," the boy continued, "Son of the Great Spirit God Jerome told about. Tree Tall did not have to go away alone to fast. Tree Tall asked and this Spirit came."

Gray Seal was shaking his head, his long black hair falling loosely around his face and shoulders. The man was once again keeping himself and his hair clean since his pride had returned. "This Jesus is the whiteskin's God. Not a good guardian for the Indian."

"Yes he is," the boy protested. "Jesus is a good guardian for all people. Tree Tall talks to him.

Prays. Jesus helps Tree Tall and his family. He gave the white store-man the idea to trade carvings of Gray Seal and baskets of Little Pine for food, tools, better clothes than the worn-out rags the soldiers bring to the reservation."

Gray Seal was still shaking his head.

The boy yearned for his father to understand. "Jesus freed Tree Tall from the white trappers when they tried to keep him as a slave. Tree Tall prayed the way Jerome said to do. The chain came off."

"You tell us the trapper not lock the chain good," Gray Seal reminded.

"But Jesus was the one who made him forget!" Tree Tall declared.

"Is the ax too heavy for the Indian boy?" It was Bright Sky, the girl he had brought back with him when he had returned to the reservation. The girl's small oval face made her dark eyes appear very large.

Tree Tall turned to watch Bright Sky and his mother walk out into the clearing. The boy sighed. Sometimes he wished he had not found this girl after the tribe who held her as a slave had gone off. Her tongue could be very sharp. He wondered if she might not be able to split logs into boards just by talking to them.

He looked at his mother. Little Pine was not tall. She was small around the waist and her black hair was long and shining. The boy had seen many white women while at Oregon City, but he thought his mother looked better in the clothes of the whites than any white woman he had seen. He was glad Jerome's father brought his family better things than the cast-off clothes the soldiers made the Indians wear.

"You have cut many boards for our new lodge," Little Pine remarked. "The tools traded to us by Jerome's father make the work go fast."

"Yes," the boy agreed, "but Gray Seal has done much. He now moves well on his leg with the help of the forked pole."

His father smiled at Little Pine. "Gray Seal feels more like a man again, here in the clearing away from other Indians and the white soldiers."

Little Pine nodded. "I talked to Spotted Elk's woman. They may build their lodge here beside us. Spotted Elk waits only to see if the soldiers let Gray Seal live here. Maybe it will be much like our old village again."

"And what does Grandmother think?" Tree Tall asked.

Little Pine sighed. "She is old. Changes are harder on the old ones. She will be happy to get away from the encampment by the river. The soldiers bring in more and more Indians. Many are long-time enemies of our tribe. White-skinned soldiers do not understand why Indians do not live as one people. Do not know of the wars between our tribes since time began."

"Here!" Bright Sky had picked up the heavy broadax and was trying to raise it over her head. "Bright Sky will show Tree Tall how to make cedar boards for new lodge." But the ax fell with a thud to the ground.

Tree Tall laughed, holding his side. "If we wait for the girl to split boards, we will spend the time of the long rains in a leaky lean-to."

Gray Seal hobbled over to Bright Sky and picked up the ax. Holding it with one hand, he brought it down hard on the wedge, completing the split Tree Tall had started.

Little Pine smiled. "It is good having Gray Seal more like the one she left her father's lodge for."

Bright Sky was not about to be put down so easily. "If Bright Sky talked all the time to the white man's Jesus God, she would have strength like the Indian boy. Jesus God gives Tree Tall magic, maybe," she said, looking at Tree Tall.

Turning to the girl, Gray Seal said, "Do not bad-talk a boy's guardian spirit. It is not good."

And so, Tree Tall thought happily, his father had accepted his Jesus guardian!

Just then they heard the sound of running horses. They turned to look toward the path that led back to the main Indian encampment. Tree Tall's heart pounded. "Soldiers come!"

They were coming fast. Before he could

14

wonder why, three horses carrying white soldiers galloped out into the clearing. A man far in front was astride a dull brown horse. It was tall and bony with a dished neck. The lead horse's long legs beat an easy rhythm as it ran effortlessly.

Two other men mounted on horses followed. One horse was a reddish brown and the other a dark bay. Both were sleek and good to look at. Tree Tall longed for such an animal. How he would love to ride a horse! The lead horse swept past followed by the other two, gone from sight along a path that led into the far trees.

"White soldiers no work," Gray Seal complained. "Make horse work instead."

"The two horses behind. They are good," Tree Tall noted.

Gray Seal nodded. "But not fast like the bony brown one. Gray Seal thinks the wind is locked in that one's heart. It breathes in the ground so fast the other two may never see it again."

That evening after eating with his family at their lean-to on the rim of the crowded Indian encampment by the river, Tree Tall wandered off toward the camp of the soldiers. It was good not to fear the taunts of the other boys of the enemy tribes as he had at first. When he returned from Oregon City—after running away partly to escape their taunts—he had helped the Indian boys learn the white man's words. One day soon all Indian children must go to the whiteskins' school, it was said, where they would talk only with the words of the whites. After Tree Tall had helped the boys learn some of these words, they had left him alone. Tree Tall had also helped his family learn to speak with the whiteskins' words. But when the whites were not around, they continued to use their own language.

Tree Tall knew Indians were not supposed to go to the soldiers' camp, but he wanted so much to see their horses up close. He had longed for a horse ever since he had seen one ridden by a warrior of a tribe that lived across the far mountains. His people, the ones who stayed close to the wide saltwaters that roared beyond the sands, had no horses.

He stopped on the outskirts of the soldiers' camp, looking toward their horses picketed under nearby trees. He did not see the dark bay, but the reddish horse was there. The ugly brown horse was there, too, standing with its head drooping, its lower lip hanging down. It seemed strange, seeing such an animal with the soldiers' good-looking horses.

Tree Tall noticed a young soldier walking toward him then. "You want something?" he asked as he drew closer.

Tree Tall shook his head. This was the man who had ridden the reddish horse past the site

16

of their new lodge. "Just like horse."

The soldier smiled. He appeared younger than the others. His hair had red streaks in it and there were tiny brown spots all over his face. The boy had never seen a whiteskin like this one. "So, you like horses," he said.

"Someday Tree Tall will have horse."

"I was just about to give mine a rubdown. Want to come along?" The man turned and started off toward the picket line. Tree Tall moved quickly to catch up. The soldier looked at the boy. "I saw you back in the clearing today. That's a good place to build a house. Did you say your name is Tree Tall?"

The boy nodded. "Soldiers say Tree Tall use white name now. Matthew Stone. Make Indians wear white man's clothes."

"I know." There was a look of understanding on the young soldier's face. "But you like your Indian things and names better."

"Tree Tall will always be Tree Tall. Not Matthew Stone."

They had reached the horses. The man went in beside the red one, leading it out to where the boy waited. "You know, Tree Tall, my name is Matthew, too. What do you think of that? Only they call me Matt for short. I don't much like the name Matthew either." He turned to rub the horse between its ears. "This is my cavalry mount. His name is Red." Matt chuckled.

17

Tree Tall was actually riding a horse for the first time. It
was even better than he had dreamed it would be.

"Guess they thought we were well matched, what with my reddish hair and freckles. Want to hold Red while I rub him down?"

The boy took the rope, reaching out to touch Red's nose in the center of the soft spot between the nostrils.

When Matt finished, he turned to the boy. "Want to sit on his back?"

"Tree Tall would like that!"

"Ever been on a horse?"

"No. Enemy tribes across the far mountains have horse. Whiteskins have horse. Not Tree Tall's people."

"Come here on Red's left side and I'll boost you up."

Suddenly the boy was astride Red's back. He could feel the animal's warm sides going in and out as it breathed. The horse stepped around and Tree Tall nearly tumbled from its back.

"Here," Matt said, "grab a handful of mane and kind of let your body go with him. I'll lead him around so you can get the feel of it."

Before long, Tree Tall relaxed. It was easy, sitting on the horse as it walked slowly behind Matt. The boy felt like a young hawk learning to fly. He was actually riding a horse for the first time. It was even better than he had dreamed it would be.

When he returned to the lean-to later, Bright Sky pointed to his pants. "You have the hair of the horse on you," she said.

Tree Tall smiled. "Ride the white soldier's horse. The horse is Red. The soldier is Matthew. He has the same name as soldiers give to Tree Tall. Together we do not like this name, so he is Matt and Tree Tall is still Tree Tall. If white soldiers ever make Tree Tall use the white name it will be Matt."

"This soldier let you ride his horse?" the girl asked.

Tree Tall nodded. "Ride again tomorrow night."

Gray Seal sat back in the shadows. But Little Pine and her mother sat close to the fire weaving their baskets by its flickering light. The older woman's long thick hair was now flecked with white, turning it the color of gray. At first she had refused to wear the whites' clothes. But Little Pine insisted. It was the only way the soldiers would give them food from the scrawny cows they brought to the reservation. But sometimes the old woman would slip out of the too-big dresses she chose for herself and put on her old woven skirt and cape, made from the soft strips of inner bark from the cedar trees. Then she would disappear into the forest alone for a time.

She looked up now. "Maybe the Indian boy's skin will bleach if he is with whites too much." Her words were cutting, not said to tease.

"No. Tree Tall is Indian for all time," the boy told her. "Learn to ride the horse now. Someday Tree Tall will have a horse."

"Humph," the old woman snorted. "Where will Tree Tall get this horse?"

"Not know. But will have a horse someday. You will see!"

Little Pine remained silent as she worked, twisting strips of dried and then dampened cat-tail leaves around and around as she made her basket. His grandmother had stopped her work. She stared off into the darkness as though in a dream. "If old woman was young again, and had horse, she would climb on its back and go far far from here. Would ride off to spirit land and never come back." Her voice trailed away. Little Pine looked at her mother.

"We will be happy again," Little Pine said, "after Gray Seal and Tree Tall have our lodge built. The clearing is only a short walk from here. It is quiet. It will be much like our old home. Spotted Elk and his woman may decide to live beside us again. Maybe others of our old village will come."

The next day Tree Tall and Gray Seal worked again on their new lodge, setting the four corner posts in place. Spotted Elk went along to help. Soon they would fit the split cedar boards solid against the posts, forming four outside walls. Later they would make a small peaked roof on top to fit over the main roof to let the smoke out, but keep the rain from getting in.

After Tree Tall had eaten the evening meal that night with his family, he started back to the soldiers' camp. Bright Sky tagged along. "Why do you follow me all the time?" Tree Tall protested. "Matt might not want you in the camp of the whites."

"Bright Sky does not want to ride the red horse. Just watch the Indian boy." She giggled. "Maybe see Indian boy fall in dust."

# 2

# Big Dreams

MATT was waiting by the horses when the Indian youngsters reached the soldiers' camp. He let Bright Sky pet Red, then helped Tree Tall upon the horse's back. Matt had put the bridle on Red this time. He showed the boy how to grip the horse with his legs. At last he handed him the long leathers connected to the bit and stood back. "Go ahead. Red will do what you want."

Tree Tall sat straight and proud. This was very close to the way he had dreamed it would be. Only the horse of his dreams was as dark as the night sky when the moon was a half curl. But for now, this was the best that had happened since he had asked the great God's Son, Jesus, to be his guardian Spirit.

Bright Sky seemed impressed with his horsemanship. Later she chattered on and on about it when the two returned to their camp fire. His family listened, but said little.

Every evening after that, Tree Tall, sometimes accompanied by Bright Sky, went to the soldiers' camp and the boy rode Red. Soon he was cantering the horse with ease, learning to command the animal with his legs and the thin leathers Matt called reins. The boy tried riding with Matt's army saddle once, but he did not like it. What he liked was the warm feel of the horse between his knees.

One evening Tree Tall asked Matt about the ugly brown horse he had seen race past their new lodge. "Other soldiers' horses look good. Why have brown horse?"

"You mean old Crow?" Matt asked with a laugh. "He's not a cavalry mount. Deke found him along the trail as we came out from the States—from the east. We figured the horse must have belonged to a settler with one of the wagon trains. At first Deke used Crow as a pack horse, until it was found he could run. Since then Deke has made money in racing Crow against the horses of settlers and other soldiers. By the looks of the old horse you'd sure never guess he could run like he does."

Matt and Tree Tall walked over to look at the brown horse. As usual Crow stood with his head down and his lower lip hanging. He was not thin, as though he had been starved. There was just no extra flesh over his big bones. His mane was wispy and his tail long and thin.

"He sure was nowhere around when the good Lord passed out pretties, was he?" Matt remarked.

By the time the boy and his father were finishing their new lodge in the clearing, Tree Tall was riding Red as though he had ridden horseback all his life. Matt's friendship had given the boy freedom to come and go in the soldiers' camp.

The soldier captain told Tree Tall one day he thought it would be good if some of the other Indian families built their lodges back away from the river, too, since so many were crowding into the main camp. The boy told this to Spotted Elk who decided he would soon start his own lodge beside that of Gray Seal's family. Tree Tall was glad.

Things seemed to be going better for everyone except his grandmother. She had been growing quieter every day. It was not like her. It was as though the fire of her spirit was about to go out. Tree Tall could tell Little Pine was worried about her mother.

The day came when their lodge was ready. They were gathering the last of their belongings to move back to the forest clearing when Tree Tall's grandmother brought a strange shaman—a medicine man—to their lean-to. The shaman's name was Two Bears. He was of their tribe, but one Tree Tall had never seen before. He was old and his hair unkempt, as was the custom with medicine men, giving them a menacing appearance.

"Many Songs said you have built a new lodge. Wants evil spirits run off before you eat—before you sleep there. Two Bears will do this now!"

Tree Tall had nearly forgotten his grandmother's name was Many Songs. The white man said her new white name must now be Lilly Smith. But to Tree Tall she would always be simply Grandmother.

Gray Seal followed the shaman back to the clearing, hobbling along with the aid of his forked pole. Tree Tall and Bright Sky walked behind Gray Seal, each carrying their own things. Behind them Little Pine and her mother carried the rest. They did not have much. They had taken some things to the lodge earlier.

When they reached the lodge Two Bears looked through the small opening and grunted. He turned to Tree Tall's grandmother and held out his hand. "Will take one good basket and one good man's shirt."

The old woman handed the shaman the basket she had recently completed, then rummaged through the pile of clothes they had brought from the lean-to. She pulled out a shirt

Gray Seal had received in trade from Jerome's father and gave it to Two Bears. Gray Seal and the others watched without protest. It was the usual way, the custom, to pay for a shaman's services.

Two Bears took the basket and shirt. He looked them over, then placed them on the ground. He began his dance, shaking a rattle made of carved wood, his singsong chant rising and falling as he circled the cedar lodge.

Bright Sky moved closer to Tree Tall and whispered, "Two Bears is very old. How can he keep on and on like that?"

She was right. The shaman was indeed old. Tree Tall glanced at his mother and grandmother. Little Pine's face was unreadable. But his grandmother's. . . . Her eyes shown with sparks of life the boy had not seen there for a long long time. Her body swayed back and forth as though she had become a part of Two Bear's ritual. Tree Tall thought of the Great Spirit God and of Jesus. He did not think they liked what was happening here. He felt the Great Spirit God, who had made all things, was probably the only one who could control the spirits of good and evil.

At last the shaman stopped. Bright Sky giggled behind her hand. Many Songs glanced at the girl with a scowl, then ran to the medicine man and dropped to her knees at his feet. She swayed back and forth, still caught up in the ritual. Two Bears placed a hand on her head and chanted for a moment. Then he stopped and walked away, disappearing into the forest walking toward the river with the basket and the shirt.

It did not take long to settle into their new lodge. Tree Tall had brought hot coals earlier from their morning fire at the lean-to. He started a new fire on the dirt floor in the center of the building. He looked around inside. It was good. It was not anything like Jerome's family lived in, but it was theirs and it was good. The best part was that he and his father had built it together, with some help at times from Spotted Elk. Tree Tall only wished they could have a window of glass, like the clear ice he had seen in the white people's houses at Oregon City.

The next morning the lodge was set in order and Tree Tall had free time at last. Little Pine allowed Bright Sky to leave her basket-weaving lessons. Together the two wandered back to the main encampment, then on to the place of the soldiers. Tree Tall had not ridden Red for days. He had been too busy helping get their lodge ready. When he and Bright Sky arrived at the soldiers' camp they found Matt and Red gone. Disappointed, the two had started back when they saw a wagon approaching along the river trail.

"It's Jerome and his father," Tree Tall exclaimed.

Bright Sky looked up. "Maybe they bring new dresses for Bright Sky, Little Pine, and grandmother Many Songs. And food!"

Tree Tall wondered if Bright Sky would ever get enough to eat. "You will be as the fat beaver if you eat all the time," he warned the girl as the blond-haired white boy and his father drew closer.

Jerome, who was a bit older than Tree Tall, saw them and waved. Tree Tall raised his own arm in welcome. He and Bright Sky raced to meet them. They crawled up on the back of the wagon as Jerome's father pulled the horses to a quick stop before going on to the soldiers' camp.

The Indian boy pointed toward the path that led to the clearing where they now lived. "Tree Tall's people back that way."

"Have you finished your house?" the black-haired white man with bushy beard asked.

Tree Tall nodded. "That way." He pointed again trying to get the man to turn the horses toward the path.

"I have to let the soldiers inspect what I've brought to trade first," he explained. "Before I leave, I have to let them see what I'm taking back to my store."

Tree Tall did not like that. Why did these white soldiers treat Indians like children? Gray

29

Seal was a man, the same as the white man.

When they reached the soldiers' camp, Jerome showed the two Indian youngsters what they had brought. There was more clothing, tools, and some cooking things for Little Pine and Many Songs. There were moccasins, too, the kind made by tribes across the far mountains.

Bright Sky was excited about the moccasins.

"Not good here," Tree Tall told her. "Too close to the wide saltwaters here. Too much rain comes down. Moccasins get stiff and hard. Better to go bare of foot like the Indian people on this side of mountains."

"We will wear them when it is not so wet," the girl retorted. "Like now, in the warm days of the sun."

"Here come some soldiers," Jerome said, looking past Tree Tall.

"Hello, there," Matt called as he rode out of the group of horsemen to stop beside the wagon. The other soldiers rode on by. "You must be the Oregon City storekeeper. Tree Tall has told me how you've helped his family."

The white man extended his hand to shake Matt's hand. "Tree Tall's family are the ones who are helping me. I've already sold most of the things they've given me in trade."

While the two men talked, Jerome and Tree Tall wandered off toward the river with Bright Sky following. "I wish you could come back to

Oregon City with us," Jerome said, picking up a small flat rock and sending it skipping across a quiet pool by the water's edge. "A settler just came from the East across the overland trail. He has some of the best horses I've ever seen. Some are a new breed started by a man in the East named Morgan. He has a stallion, too. It's half Morgan and half Thoroughbred. I've never seen it run, but he says it's real fast."

"Tree Tall ride friend Matt's horse. Ride fast now. Not fall off. Matt says Tree Tall is like born on horse's back."

"You sure ought to come to the race then." Jerome told Tree Tall about the settler's challenge as Bright Sky listened. "If anyone beats his stallion in a race through the forest, he will give them one of his bred mares. Wouldn't that be something!"

"Tree Tall would like to see this." He thought for a moment. "Maybe Matt would let Tree Tall ride Red in the race. Get mare from settler."

Jerome laughed. "I don't think the captain would let you ride a cavalry horse in a race."

The Indian boy was pulling at Jerome's arm. "Come. Find Matt!"

The girl finally spoke. "Think Indian boy dream too big dreams."

Jerome and Bright Sky followed as Tree Tall ran back to talk to Matt. Jerome's father listened as the boy told the white soldier about the horse race, adding how he would like to ride Red so he could win the mare for himself.

Matt turned to Jerome's father. "Is he right about the race?"

"That's what I hear," the bearded man noted.

Matt was thoughtful for a time. At last he turned to Tree Tall. "I couldn't let you ride Red. He belongs to the United States government, not to me. Besides, Red's not a fast horse. But what about Crow? He's just a stray. If the captain would let us go to Oregon City, I'll bet Deke would enter Crow in the race. Maybe I can talk him into letting you ride. You're a whole lot better horseman already than Deke will ever be."

The Indian boy's eyes shone with excitement. "Win mare for Tree Tall to keep?"

"I don't know about that," Matt hedged. "But we can ask."

They went with Matt to find Deke. He was sitting outside one of the tents rubbing oil on a boot. He appeared to be about Gray Seal's age. His middle was thickset and there was a natural slope to his shoulders. He mopped his forehead as he listened to Matt and Jerome's father tell of the race that would soon take place at Oregon City.

Deke glanced at Tree Tall when Matt told about the boy wanting to ride Crow. "Not a bad idea," he commented with a slow drawl. "I've seen the Indian kid ride. He's good. And he's light. But I don't know if he and Crow would get along. That old horse has a mind of his own."

"We could try him. I think the captain would let us go," Matt said.

Deke smiled. "He just might want to go along!"

Matt acted as though he was at the end of his talk with Deke and was about to turn away. Tree Tall pulled his arm. "Ask Deke about mare."

"Oh, yeah." Matt smiled. "The boy wants a horse of his own in the worst way. He'd like to keep the prize mare for himself if he wins."

"No way!" Deke said with a shake of his head.

The boy folded his arms across his chest, thrusting out his jaw. "Then Tree Tall not ride Crow."

Deke eyed him, then looked at Jerome's father. "You say this settler's stallion is fast?"

"That's what he says. The horse looks like he can run."

"What's the settler makin' out of it?"

"The way I understand it, he's putting up fifty dollars besides the mare. All the others who enter pay twenty dollars. The winner gets it all. So if the settler wins, he takes the money and keeps his mare."

"And so," Deke noted, "if another horse beats this stallion, the owner gets the mare, the settler's fifty, and all the money paid by those who entered the race?"

"That's what I've heard."

Matt was shaking his head. "That settler fella must feel pretty sure of himself and his stallion."

Jerome's father nodded. "That's about what it comes down to. There's already six men I know who've entered. That's one hundred and twenty dollars right there, not counting the settler's fifty."

Matt turned back to Deke. "Tree Tall is light, so Crow wouldn't have much weight to hold him back."

Deke looked at Tree Tall again. "Tell you what, kid. If you ride Crow and win that race, here's what I'll do. I'll keep the money and you can have the mare for awhile. But only until after her foal is born. Soon as it's weaned, I get the mare back and you can keep the foal. I've got no way to care for it anyway. How's that sound?"

Tree Tall's eyes flashed. He stepped forward and stuck out his hand the way he had seen Jerome's father do. Deke took the boy's offered hand and they gave one solemn shake up and then down.

Matt was smiling. "It looks as though we'd better get busy. But first we need permission from the captain to train for the race and to take Tree Tall to Oregon City. Not to mention bein' able to go there ourselves."

# 3

# Getting Ready

THE CAPTAIN agreed to their plans to enter the race. Matt, Deke, and Tree Tall then went to where Crow was tied. Jerome, his father, and Bright Sky followed. They stood looking at the long-legged brown horse. No one would ever have guessed the horse had a heart to run.

Deke started to saddle the big-boned gelding for Tree Tall to ride, but Matt advised against it. "The boy's used to riding bareback. He sticks like glue to Red."

Crow stood quiet as Deke gave the boy a boost up. The ground seemed farther away from Crow's back then it did from Red's. Tree Tall could feel the horse's ribs against his knees as Deke handed him the reins.

"Now with this animal, kid, you've got to keep a loose rein. He don't like being held uptight at the mouth. It's just natural for him to keep his head low. Trouble is, when he gets to runnin' he's sometimes hard to stop. I've had to run him into the brush a couple of times. Other times he stops soon as you pull leather."

Tree Tall ran his hand along Crow's thin neck. The horse quivered. Deke pushed the boy's hand away. "He don't much like bein' petted."

"Tree Tall will ride Crow at a walk first," the boy suggested.

Jerome and his father watched with Bright Sky as Tree Tall nudged Crow into a walk with his bare heels. Deke and Matt stood back giving the horse room to move out. Crow's gait was easy at a walk. Tree Tall turned him first one way and then the other as Matt had taught him to do with Red. Crow responded well to the reins, carrying his head low as if only half-awake. After several times around, the boy squeezed his legs and thumped Crow's ribs with his heels. The horse swung off immediately to a rocky trot. Tree Tall gripped harder with his legs to keep in place over the horse's sharp backbone.

Suddenly Crow came to life. With a lunge he took off at full gallop. Tree Tall pulled hard on the reins, but Crow did not slow. They were headed toward the Indian encampment. Crow ran with a speed Tree Tall had never before known. Not even in the big canoe as it rode the

36

breakers of the wide saltwaters beyond the sands.

Somehow the horse angled his long body through the Indian camp without knocking over anything or anyone. Tree Tall bent low along Crow's skinny neck, trying to keep from falling. Ahead, beyond the many camp fires, was a path into the forest opposite the one leading to the clearing and their lodge. Tree Tall knew this path to be littered with brush and fallen trees. But he made up his mind Crow would not be rid of him so easily!

He felt the horse's body lift into the air. The sound of hooves on hard-packed earth stopped. The boy looked down. They were sailing over a fallen tree, coming down with a jolt on the other side.

After that he could not think. He hung on, waiting to be thrown from the running horse. Tree limbs scraped his back, tearing his shirt. Sweat from Crow's body stung Tree Tall's legs, the wispy mane feathering across the boy's face.

At last the horse slowed. Tree Tall had given up pulling on the reins, thinking only of staying on the animal's back. Now he pulled back and began talking. "Easy, Crow. Whoa, boy." These were words he had heard Matt talk to Red. "Whoa. . . . Easy!" Slowly the horse responded. At last Tree Tall had him back to a rough trot. Crow was breathing hard. Tree Tall was shaking. Was it worth it riding this horse in a race? Was it worth risking his life for a horse of his own?

"Yes," he answered aloud. "Tree Tall will learn to ride Crow." He touched the brown animal's neck. "Crow will get the horse, the foal of the mare, for Tree Tall. He will win money and the mare for Deke."

Just then Matt and Deke galloped up on their army horses. Together the three headed back to camp, where Tree Tall found Bright Sky had been crying. He could tell by the clean streaks on her oval face. Jerome and his father looked relieved to see him.

"Indian boy show off, Bright Sky think," the girl pouted up at him. "Next time Bright Sky will not watch!"

Deke stepped down from his horse to feel Crow's legs. "He seems all right. Guess it didn't hurt him."

"I'm a bit more concerned about the boy," said the bearded store-man. "Are you all right, Tree Tall?"

The Indian boy nodded.

Matt dismounted from Red to help Tree Tall down from Crow's back. "We've got a lot of work to do before you're ready to enter a race."

Tree Tall smiled. "Maybe we teach horse to whoa?"

"I think you have another road to cross before

38

Tree Tall rides in any race," Jerome's father noted. "No one has bothered to ask his parents."

"No problem," Deke said. "If the captain says he can ride, then he can ride. Indians don't have much say around here."

"They have a say with me!" the store-man said. "You either talk to them, or I'll ask your captain to reconsider."

Deke finally agreed. Jerome's father needed to see Gray Seal anyway, and so they all walked to the clearing together.

Little Pine seemed worried when told of the race. But pride was reflected in Gray Seal's dark eyes. He looked at his son. Tree Tall's grandmother watched without a word. Gray Seal listened to their race plans and the promise of the foal if Tree Tall and Crow won.

The Indian man spoke to the boy in their own words so the whites could not understand. "Tree Tall will be wealthy in the eyes of our people if he wins the horse. We will all hold our heads up. Will walk as proud Indians again."

So it was decided and the plans were made. Tree Tall and Crow would enter the Oregon City race in just three weeks. Gray Seal and Little Pine would travel with the soldiers and Tree Tall to the white man's village. Many Songs and Bright Sky would stay behind to look after their lodge.

Gray Seal gave the boy more freedom to ride

"Tree Tall will be wealthy in the eyes of our people if he wins
the horse," Gray Seal said. "We will walk
as proud Indians again."

Crow as the days grew closer to the race. Their lodge was now finished and Gray Seal was able to do much more than he had before. Bright Sky watched whenever she could get away, even though she had said she would not. Deke and Matt had marked out a course through the forest, making a wide swing along the outskirts of camp. They rode over it with Tree Tall several times, until the boy felt comfortable enough to lope Crow by himself, never allowing him to run as at first.

"You've got to let the horse know you're in control," Matt told him. "As soon as he realizes that, you'll be able to let him out."

After finally running Crow at full gallop one evening, Tree Tall returned the brown horse to the picket line. He began rubbing the tall animal's hide dry as Matt had shown him, using a handful of dry grass.

Bright Sky walked up as Tree Tall stretched to reach Crow's back. "You like this horse, Bright Sky think."

"Tree Tall likes all horses. But will like best the foal Crow will win for Tree Tall."

"How do you know you win?"

"Talk to the great God's Son Jesus. Tell Him Tree Tall wants the horse very much."

"How do you know there is such a god?"

The boy turned to the girl. They were alone at the long line of horses. "Tree Tall knows. Feels

41

Spirit of God inside." He struck his chest with a fist. "Tree Tall is a Christ-follower now. A Christian, Jerome calls it."

"Bright Sky does not know this white man's God," the girl remarked.

Tree Tall shook his head. "He is not only the white man's God. He is God of all people. All things."

She was looking earnestly into the boy's face. "Could the Great Spirit God help Bright Sky?"

"If Bright Sky asks God's Son Jesus to forgive her for the bad things she does."

"Would Bright Sky then get things she asks for?"

The boy seemed uncertain. "Not sure. . . . " He recalled how he and his people had been made to come to the reservation. He had been angry with God then. But now things were better for them. God had given him what he had asked for, only it had taken longer than he had wanted and it had happened in a different way. Now, if he could win the foal, he would know for sure God answered prayer.

When it was time at last to leave for the whiteskins' village, it had been decided Bright Sky could go along. She whispered to Tree Tall as they climbed onto the wagon the soldier captain let Matt use to take Tree Tall's family over the mountains. "Great Spirit God listen to Bright Sky, too, maybe."

Deke rode his army horse. Crow was tied to the back of the wagon along with Matt's horse. Matt drove the team with Gray Seal bouncing along on the high seat beside him. Tree Tall, Little Pine, and Bright Sky sat in back of the wagon with their baskets of food, sleeping robes, and an army tent Matt had brought along for them to use. Matt said they would set the tent up behind Jerome's house, while he and Deke stayed at a place he called a hotel.

The four-day trip was enjoyable. Even Little Pine appeared happy. It was good being away from the reservation. But still, whenever anyone spoke of the upcoming race, Tree Tall's mother became very quiet. The boy knew she worried.

Tree Tall could tell his mother and father were nervous about visiting the white man's village. He and Bright Sky told them all they could of the wide road with tall houses painted white. And of the stores and the white man's things that could be traded for something they called money. They told, too, of the sawmill Tree Tall had as yet not seen—a mill that cut logs into smooth boards. The round blade was somehow pushed by the power of the fast-tumbling waterfall from the nearby river.

On the fourth day they came to a wide main road the whites called a street. This was Oregon City. It was busy that day with horses, wagons, and people going back and forth. A high cliff rose behind the buildings on one side of the street, while the river bordered the back of the buildings on the opposite side. Jerome had told Tree Tall the white men called this river the Willamette.

Little Pine scrunched down in the wagon to hide from the stares of the whiteskins. But Gray Seal sat tall and proud on the high wagon seat. When Matt stopped the team in front of the store, Tree Tall and Bright Sky scrambled down and ran inside. The bearded store-man appeared glad to see them, coming out to direct Matt to his house near the other end of the dusty street.

Deke had stopped to talk to some men by a rail where people tied their horses. He then rode up to the wagon. "There's eight signed up and paid their twenty dollars for the race. Soon as I get our name on that list, there'll be ten of us, countin' the settler." Deke glanced at Tree Tall. "That's two hundred and thirty dollars if Crow wins, besides the mare and the foal you want. But it could mean a lot of jostling at the start with that many horses entered." He turned to Matt. "We'd better show the kid how to handle himself in case someone tries takin' advantage."

Matt nodded. "Good idea. I'll drive the wagon down to the house and help set up the tent. Then I'll take the team to the stable. We can start working with Tree Tall and Crow in the morning."

Deke untied the two saddle horses from the back so Matt could drive the team and wagon to Jerome's house.

By now Gray Seal and Little Pine were able to speak the white words fairly well. It made it easier when Jerome's mother greeted them and then showed Little Pine through the house. Gray Seal refused to go inside the white man's building. As Tree Tall had thought, the thing his mother liked best was the window with the ice-like glass you could see through.

The race was still a few days away, giving Tree Tall time to learn the course. Since Jerome's sister took up much of Bright Sky's time, Tree Tall was free to be with Jerome in the evenings.

They stayed close to Jerome's house, however, after some white boys aimed insulting remarks in Tree Tall's direction when they overheard him call Oregon City a village.

"This ain't no Indian village," jeered one. "This here is a town."

It was the second evening and Jerome and Tree Tall were sitting on the front porch steps. The boys who had made fun of Tree Tall hovered a short distance away.

Tree Tall had been watching them. He did not like being laughed at. "Do white boys make trouble for Jerome?" he asked.

"Not usually. They just don't understand Indians. They think it's strange you're my friend."

"Does Jerome want to fight these boys? Tree Tall will help."

Jerome was shaking his head. "No. It would probably just make things worse. My father showed me in the Bible where Jesus said we should do good to our enemies and love our neighbor as ourselves."

"What is Bible?" Tree Tall asked. "And what is neighbor?"

"A neighbor can be anyone. Come on." Jerome led the Indian boy into the house to a thick stack of papers on a table. They were covered with black leather on the top and the bottom. "This is a book. It's a Bible," Jerome explained as he handed it to Tree Tall. "Words are written on the paper we can read and understand. It's God's Word to us."

Tree Tall frowned, opening the top to look at the black marks on the paper pages. "Read? How is this done?"

"Those are words. We read them with our eyes instead of speaking them with our mouths."

"How you hear words that come off paper and not out of mouth?"

"We learn what each word means. Then when we look at a word we hear it in our mind as though someone was talking. We can speak them out loud, too, so others hear the words."

The wonder of it! Tree Tall had no idea there could be such a thing in the whole forest land and the saltwaters beyond. Words on paper your eyes heard in your mind! This was indeed a marvel. How he would like to do that.

"Tonight," Jerome was saying, "my father will read out loud from the Bible. Would you and Bright Sky like to come hear him read God's Word?"

Tree Tall nodded.

Later, after Little Pine had cooked their evening meal of roots and dried beef by a small cooking fire outside the army tent, Tree Tall motioned for Bright Sky to come with him. He knocked at the back door of Jerome's house, the way the white woman had said he should do before entering.

Jerome's father smiled at the Indian children. "Sit here at the table with us. Jerome told me you might come."

Tree Tall looked with longing at the thick book in front of the man. "How you know words on paper?"

"That's what you'll be learning when you go to the white man's school. I hear it will soon be ready."

The boy frowned. "Not sure Tree Tall want to go to this school. It is said we can no more talk

47

our own words there. This is not right. Why are white words better than Indian words?"

The man seemed a bit sad. "I understand your feelings, but there are so many different languages—words, as you call them—spoken by the local Indians. It would be impossible to teach anything unless only one language was used. And yet, I do not fully agree with the way my people are going about this."

# 4

# Threat of the Stallion

TREE TALL did not like the thought of being forced to speak with only the whiteskins' words at this school he kept hearing about. He did not like that at all! And yet, it would be like having great power, like that of a shaman, to look at a paper and hear words in his head, or to talk them right off the paper to someone else.

Before Jerome's father read from the Bible he first put his chin down close to his chest as Tree Tall had seen him do many times before. He then talked to the Great Spirit God and to Jesus. At last he looked up. "Jerome said he told you of Jesus' teaching about loving our neighbor as ourselves."

The Indian boy nodded. "Not easy, Tree Tall think."

"That's right," the bearded white man agreed.

"And we couldn't do it without Jesus' help. Sometimes I have to tell Jesus he needs to love people through me because I cannot." The man opened the black book. "I thought I'd read that part tonight." He began then reading from a place toward the back of the book.

Many strange words came to Tree Tall's ears. He glanced at Bright Sky. She, too, seemed not to understand. Finally the white man stopped. "This is the story of a man who came to Jesus asking what he needed to do to have God accept him in his kingdom. Jesus asked the man if he knew what was written in the law. The man said it was written that he should love God above all things and love his neighbor as he loved himself."

Tree Tall was shaking his head. "Very hard words. How can Tree Tall love ones who hurt him—like the white soldiers who make us live on reservation land, or boys of enemy tribes who fight?"

"Tell about the good Samaritan," Jerome prodded.

His father smiled. "I was just about to. You see, Tree Tall, there was a man Jesus told about who was hurt and left to die at the side of the road by some bad men. People passed by the injured man, but no one stopped to help. Then another, who was a Samaritan, came by. He stopped and took care of the man who was hurt.

Jesus used this story to show we are to help others. You see, the man who was injured was a Jew. Jews hated Samaritans, as many white men seem to hate Indians. It would be like you finding a white man and helping him even though he, or his people, had said or done hurtful things to you."

Tree Tall was shaking his head. "Very hard story."

"Yes," Jerome's father agreed, "but Jesus ended by saying we should go and do the same to others."*

The Indian boy decided he would have to think about that. He was not sure how he felt about loving others as he loved himself. Sometimes he did not love himself at all. How could he be kind to someone who was not kind to him? Yes, he would have to think much about that in the hours at night before sleep came to him. It might take many such nights of sleepless thought.

The next morning Matt rode up to Jerome's house on Red, coming around to the back where the tent was set up. He was leading Crow. "You ready to ride over the race course?" he asked the Indian boy.

Gray Seal reached for the forked pole he used to help him walk. "Go watch boy ride horse," his

*Luke 10:25-37

51

father declared, getting to his feet.

But Matt was shaking his head. "You'd better stay here," the young red-haired soldier said. "Deke and I will be out on the trail with Tree Tall. There won't be anyone on the street who knows you. A lot of people here don't trust Indians."

"Gray Seal not trust whiteskins." He touched his crippled leg. "Whiteskins shoot with long stick."

"I know," Matt said. "But it wouldn't be good for you out on the street without one of us. Someone may get the idea you broke off the reservation and try to take you back tied hand and foot."

"No tie Gray Seal! Ever!" the Indian man declared. But he appeared doubtful. "Will stay. Watch over Little Pine and Bright Sky." With that he sat down again beside the fire.

It felt good to Tree Tall, being mounted on Crow again, riding beside Matt down the white man's road they called a street. At first.... Then he noticed people pointing and laughing. He turned to Matt. "They laugh at Tree Tall?"

"No. They're laughing at Crow. They know our plans to enter the race. You have to admit he's a sorry-looking horse."

Tree Tall grinned. "They soon get very big surprise, Tree Tall think!"

"I sure hope so," Matt said.

Deke was waiting on his horse in front of the store of Jerome's father. A rather stout boy, a little older than Tree Tall, was there with a man of bulky proportions. The man held the lead rope of a trim, shapely horse. It was as black as the night river. Sun rays highlighted its body as the night moon reflected off quiet waters. Its head was small, its neck thick, crested with a heavy mane of waves. The horse's ears pointed forward watching everything. His legs were slender beneath a solid body. This was the horse Tree Tall had dreamed of. The very one!

"That's the settler and his son, and the stallion Crow will have to race," Deke remarked as Tree Tall and Matt stopped their horses beside him. "I'm beginning to wish we hadn't entered this race. The stallion is half Thorough-bred. It looks like he was born to run."

"Is that like horse Tree Tall will win for Deke?" the boy asked.

"No," Matt said. "The mare is at the stable. We'll stop so you can have a look if you want." Matt was smiling, knowing full well that was exactly what Tree Tall wanted.

The boy did not understand what a "stable" was, but he soon found out. It was a big lodge-like building where horses were kept. The three dismounted and went inside. There Tree Tall saw the mare the settler would give the winner of the race. She was a dark bay, built a little like the stallion, with a thick neck and heavy black mane. Her belly bulged with the foal she carried inside.

"Good horse," Tree Tall said. "But Tree Tall dream of black horse."

"She's bred to that black stallion out there," Matt remarked. "So it's possible the foal will have the stallion's coloring."

Tree Tall nodded, looking at the mare. He turned to Deke. "Soon you have brown mare. Tree Tall have black foal."

Deke did not seem encouraged. "I just wish I'd seen that stallion before I paid my twenty dollars. Crow's fast. But I have a feelin' that black is faster. A couple other horses entered in the race look pretty good too." He shook his head, staring at the mare. "I don't believe that settler would have put this mare up as part of the winnings if he really thought he'd lose her. Don't know why I didn't think that out before. She's too valuable a horse."

"You like to have?" Tree Tall asked.

"I would.... But I'm not sure I will."

The boy stood tall. He had grown much during the past year. "Tree Tall will win mare for Deke!"

Back outside they mounted and rode west out of town. Deke told them the race course was marked with wooden stakes. Leaving the road, they followed the stakes along a path that

54

turned first south and then east, circling the high cliff that edged the town opposite the river. The path had been recently widened in places, but it would still allow only two side-by-side horses at the same time. In some places there was room for only one horse. It went up over hills that would fast steal the wind from a hard-running horse, and then down where a less than surefooted animal could fall. There were tight turns and switchbacks, too.

A chill gripped Tree Tall. He could well imagine the danger of racing full speed over such a course. It would even be worse with horses and riders jostling each other.

By now Crow responded well to the Indian boy. But unless he was running, there was simply no life to the brown horse. They reentered Oregon City from the opposite direction. Tree Tall was several yards behind the two soldiers. Crow's head was low, swinging back and forth as he walked, his lower lip drooping. Some white boys pointed and laughed. Tree Tall's face burned hot. He was glad his skin was reddish already or else they would see his embarrassment. It made him long even more for a horse of his own. When the foal he wanted was grown, no one would laugh as he rode by.

That evening Jerome took Tree Tall and Bright Sky to the river to see the sawmill. Later Jerome's father came with Gray Seal. Tree

Tall's father was impressed by the big round saw with its belts and pulleys that made the blade whirl fast through the logs.

The men and the youngsters walked back together. They stopped at the store and the white man unlocked the door so Gray Seal could see the things Tree Tall and Bright Sky had told him about.

Gray Seal pointed to a table near a high counter. "Indians make."

Sure enough, there were Little Pine's baskets and Gray Seal's wood carvings. There were moccasins made by tribes across the far mountains, too, as well as other Indian trade items. The white man explained he sent some Indian crafts by ship on the big waters around a distant point of land to the white man's towns on the East Coast.

A day passed. The settler had taken his horses and left, saying he would return the day before the race. It was just three days away. The others entered in the race were there now. Tree Tall met several on the race trail as he loped Crow over the path, allowing both himself and the horse to become accustomed to the dangerous course.

Then, two days before the race, the cavalry captain and some soldiers rode into town. Tree Tall had just returned from loping Crow along the forest race path. He pulled Crow to a stop in front of the stable where Deke and Matt waited.

Deke grinned at the captain as he and the other soldiers rode up. "I had a feelin' you'd be coming in sometime before the race."

The captain smiled in Tree Tall's direction. "How about it, boy? Think you have a chance to win this race?"

The boy nodded. "Tree Tall win race!"

"Anyone takin' bets?" a soldier asked.

"The blacksmith down the street," Deke told him.

Tree Tall looked at Matt. "What is bets?"

"That," Matt remarked with a grin, "is white man's foolishness. They give their money to someone to keep until after the race, naming the horse they think will win. That's what we call making a bet. If their choice wins, they get back more money than they bet. If the horse they named does not win, they get nothing and lose it all."

"If Tree Tall had money he would name Crow to win!" the boy declared.

"You that sure of yourself?" the captain asked.

"Tree Tall sure. Win money and bay mare for Deke. Win foal for Tree Tall."

"Come on," a soldier called, turning his horse toward the blacksmith shop. "That's all I need to hear. I'm goin' to put all I've got on old Crow. I've seen that nag run."

"Yeah, I've lost bettin' against him," another commented as he turned his horse to follow. "I'll not be makin' the same mistake again."

"Hey," Deke called after them as they headed off toward the blacksmith shop. "You've never even seen the settler's stallion. I'm having doubts about Crow myself."

But the others would not listen. They had been deceived by Deke before. "You just want us to bet on that settler's horse so the odds will be better for you," a man called back.

"But I'm not bettin' a cent, boys," Deke replied. "Honest!"

Tree Tall told Jerome about the soldiers betting on Crow and what had been said. Jerome appeared worried. "You and Crow better win that race," the white boy remarked. "Otherwise they'll sure be mad."

Tree Tall had not thought about that. It was true. There was now even more reason for him and Crow to win.

The next day the settler came back to town. He was riding the black stallion and leading the bay mare. The settler's son rode beside his father on a sorrel. A third rider, a man of slight build, was with them leading a gray and a young blackish brown horse. Jerome and Tree Tall sat on the wooden platform in front of the store watching the three horsemen. Bright Sky was with the boys. Jerome's mother had

58

brought Little Pine to the store that afternoon. The two women were inside looking at the things Tree Tall had at first found so fascinating.

Bright Sky stared at the settler's horses. She sucked in her breath. "Tree Tall ride Crow against that big black horse the fat man rides?"

Tree Tall and Jerome nodded as one.

"Bright Sky think Indian boy dream too big dreams again."

Jerome's sister came out of the store. Soon she and Bright Sky wandered off. But Tree Tall was watching the settler and the boy who had dismounted. The other man still sat on his horse. They were talking to a group of men. Deke and some of the other soldiers joined them. Tree Tall wondered what the soldiers thought after seeing the stallion. Were they sorry they had named Crow to win?

Jerome got to his feet. "Let's go hear what's going on."

The two boys stood at the edge of the gathering, listening to the settler brag how fast his stallion was. Tree Tall wished he could get close enough to at least touch this horse of his dreams. How good it would be to sit on the stallion's back.

"You ridin' that stallion yourself in the race?" a soldier was asking.

"No. I've got a man to do that. He's ridden

races back east, so he knows all the tricks to the trade."

Tricks? Tree Tall did not like the word or the smile on the settler's face. Was there a plan to make sure the black stallion would win?

# 5

# Plot of the Soldiers

"THIS RACE better be on the up and up," a soldier remarked. "We've got money on it."

"Yeah," another spoke. "Who is this who's riding for you, anyway? I'd like to talk to him!"

"He's right here," the settler said, turning to the one who had just ridden into town with him and his son. The man stepped down from his horse. He was short and very thin. He took the horses of the settler and the boy, leading the six away. Deke said something to a couple soldiers and they ran to catch up with the settler's rider. Together they walked toward the stable.

There was much activity going on all the time. It freed Tree Tall and Jerome from the threat of the boys of the town since they had other things now with which to occupy themselves.

The white boy and the Indian boy wandered back along the street later that night. Loud talk and laughter was coming from one of the buildings Jerome called a saloon.

"They drink a strong drink in there," Jerome said. "After a time it makes men act like children, only worse."

That seemed strange to Tree Tall. Why would a man want to act like a child?

Just then the door to the saloon opened and some soldiers came out with the short thin man who was to ride the settler's stallion. They were all laughing. One of the soldiers had his arm draped over the thin man's shoulder. Jerome glanced at Tree Tall, but neither spoke.

The next day, the day before the race, Tree Tall again rode Crow over the race course. This time Deke told him to let Crow out at full gallop. They were up early before anyone else was around. Deke told Matt he did not want the others to see Crow run until the race. Tree Tall wished the white people of the town could see how fast Crow was so they would stop laughing, even when they saw Tree Tall without the horse, since they knew the Indian boy was to ride Crow in the race.

Again that night the two boys wandered down the street. And again they saw soldiers come out of the saloon with the settler's rider. Only this time they were carrying the man.

"Is he dead?" Tree Tall wondered aloud. "He looks dead."

Jerome was shaking his head. "Probably drunk. I'm glad my father doesn't drink liquor like that."

Tree Tall found it hard to sleep that night. Other nights he had thought of the things Jerome's father had read from the Bible book, about loving others as ourselves. But on this night the race was the only thing on the boy's mind. He must win! But it did not seem as certain as it had before they left the reservation—before seeing the stallion. He prayed that Jesus would help him and Crow win—would help them so he could have a horse of his own.

As soon as Tree Tall had eaten the morning meal outside the tent, he and Jerome, followed by Bright Sky, went down the street to see what was going on. The race was not planned until much later in the day. People had come from all around. There were many more soldiers now. Children played in the street dodging the horses and wagons that came and went. Some men were marking off a line for the start of the race. Long poles had been set up on either side of the street with a rope that ran from top to top. Hanging from the rope was a banner of many colors.

Jerome's father was busy in his store. The three children hung around outside watching everything. It was then they saw him—the settler—walking down the center of the street. He appeared angry. He was waving his arms around as he walked. His son was beside him. Some men followed.

"They did it on purpose! I know they did!" the settler was shouting. "They got him drunk so he couldn't ride today."

"Maybe he'll feel better in time for the race," the man's son said.

The stout settler stopped, glaring at his son. "We wouldn't have a chance with that man riding our stallion. He can't even sit up!"

Jerome looked at Tree Tall. "You and Crow may just have a chance to win after all."

"Soldiers do something to the small man to help Crow win?"

"It's possible," Jerome said.

The girl looked first at Tree Tall and then Jerome. "Bright Sky prayed for Tree Tall and Crow last night."

"Come on," Jerome said. "We'd better find Matt and Deke and tell them."

But when they found the two men they learned Deke already knew what had happened. He was laughing. "The boys did all right!"

So, Tree Tall thought, it was true. The soldiers had made the settler's rider drink too much white man's strong stuff. It did not, however, make Tree Tall feel better about the race.

Matt sighed. "Deke, I don't like it. It's not going to help anyway. He's sure to find someone to ride his stallion."

"But it won't be someone who knows as much about racing," said Deke.

The three children followed Matt and Deke back up the street to find out what was happening. It was then they learned who would be riding the stallion in the race. It would be the settler's son Tom.

Bright Sky went into the store as Tree Tall and Jerome walked over to where the white boy stood alone. "Hi. I'm Jerome. Guess we've never talked before. My father owns the store here."

Tom looked to be a little older than Tree Tall. He was pudgy, but not nearly as stout as his father. The sandy-haired boy nodded. "Your father may own the store, but mine has the best horses in the whole Willamette Valley."

"I don't doubt it," said Jerome. "This is Tree Tall. He lives on the reservation. He's riding one of the soldier's horses in the race this afternoon."

Tom briefly glanced at them. "Then the Indian had better look good at my face now, 'cause he's not likely to see much of it after the race starts."

"You have good horse," Tree Tall admitted. "But Crow is fast. Maybe soon Tree Tall will have the foal from bay mare."

The settler's son turned to look again at the Indian boy. "You talk pretty big for an Indian."

Tree Tall looked deep into the white boy's blue eyes. There was much pride there. But he saw something else, too. Was it fear? Was it fear of the race they would soon run?

Tom turned then, walking away with a swagger. Was he trying to cover his fear of what lay before them out there on the forest race course? If so, Tree Tall knew how the white boy felt, for he was feeling the same churning in his stomach, the same tightness in his chest. Anything could happen out there. Anything. . . .

As the afternoon race drew nearer, the contestants began gathering on the dusty street. Some had good-looking horses. Others were not so good to look at, but all appeared able to run. Crow would stand out among such horses like a dead cedar in a grove of green. Deke had said he would bring Crow out at the last minute before time to line up. Deke's plan was to ride the brown horse himself behind the stable to warm Crow's blood and get his legs ready to run. Then when Tree Tall mounted the horse later, Crow would hopefully run faster with the boy's lighter weight.

A man climbed onto a wagon and called for the riders and owners to come forward to choose a number for their position at the start of the race. Matt went with Tree Tall and Jerome to

66

stand beside Deke. Most of the owners and riders appeared to be settlers. There were two trappers from across the Columbia River to the north who Jerome said were quartered at the Hudson's Bay Company fort called Vancouver. Jerome said they were British. But that meant nothing to Tree Tall.

An upside-down hat was passed around. When it came to Deke he pulled out a piece of paper. Something was written on it. Deke frowned. "Looks as though you'll be in line right beside that black stallion, Tree Tall."

The boy glanced up. The settler's son was standing close by looking at him. "You ever raced a horse before?" Tom asked.

"No race, till now," Tree Tall replied.

"Me neither. . . ."

"You ride around path where we race?"

"Not the last few days. But I helped my father stake it out last week."

"It has many ups, many down," Tree Tall noted. "Crooked places. Places where horse run into other horses. Not good."

"What's the matter? You scared?" the boy taunted.

Again Tree Tall thought he saw fear in the white boy's face. But it was difficult to see past the jeering words. Maybe it was his own fear looking back from Tom's blue-colored eyes. "Tree Tall want to win horse."

"You can forget about that," Tom told him. "My father wouldn't put that mare up as part of the prize if he really thought he'd lose her. Can't you see that? There's no way you're going to get that mare!"

"Come on," Matt urged, pulling Tree Tall away from the crowd around the wagon.

Jerome followed as they walked toward the stable. "I've been thinking," Jerome said to Matt. "Why don't you let Tree Tall wear a loincloth like he used to wear before the Indians were made to wear clothes like ours? He'd have a better leg grip on Crow without pants, since he's riding bareback."

"Tree Tall would like that," the Indian boy remarked with a smile.

Matt glanced at the boys. "Not a bad idea. But where would we find a loincloth?"

"My father has some soft tanned elk hide in the back of the store. Maybe he'd let us have some of it. At least a piece off the end. Want me to go ask?"

"Okay," said Matt. "See what you can do. We'll be at the stable."

When Matt and Tree Tall reached the large building where the horses were kept, they found the double doors wide open. They were walking toward the opening when the settler came out leading a couple horses—the gray one and the dusty black horse he had brought to town earlier. Both were geldings. The black had touches of brown around his nose and ears, with his black color shading to a brownish dust across his shoulders and sides.

"What you got there?" Matt asked, looking at the animals.

The plump man stopped and glared at Matt. "Are you one of those soldiers who got my rider drunk last night?"

"No, sir!" Matt replied. "I sure wasn't a part of that. I don't agree with what happened."

The settler's expression relaxed. He looked at Tree Tall then. "I understand you're to ride that brown crowbait in there."

Tree Tall nodded and smiled. "You know Crow's name?"

"It figures." The man smiled in spite of himself.

"Crow will win race, maybe. Get money and your mare for Deke. Get foal for Tree Tall."

"Don't count on it, son." The settler's tone had softened.

Matt ran a hand along the neck of the black gelding. "You've got some good horses. What's the breeding of this one?"

"His mama was a bay saddle mare of no special account. But his daddy's my stallion. He favors the stud, I think. He's just a two-year-old."

"How'd you manage to bring such horses

69

across the plains? It's a wonder the Indians didn't run them off."

"They tried," the settler admitted. "I lost a couple. But I've got my stallion and a few Morgan mares left, so I hope to soon have a sizable herd again. You wouldn't be interested in buying this black or the gray would you?"

"Wish I could. But I've got no money," Matt said.

"I know the feelin'," the fleshy man replied. "I'm going to try to sell one of these horses today. I need the money to pay off some debts I've run up."

Tree Tall was looking at the two-year-old blackish gelding. Maybe the bay mare in the stable—the one he hoped to win—would have such a foal. He reached out to touch the gelding's shoulder. The animal quivered. While this one was not the deep black of the stallion, it came very close to the color of his dream horse.

"Very good horse, Tree Tall think."

There was an expression on the settler's face of—what was it Jerome's father had talked about the last time he was here in Oregon City? Respect! Yes, there was a look of respect for the Indian boy on the settler's face.

"You've got a good eye for horses," the man said.

"And," Matt spoke up, "he's mighty good on top of one, too."

70

There was a look of respect for the Indian boy on the settler's face. "You've got a good eye for horses," the man said.

"He must be," the settler said with a laugh, "to be expected to make that bundle of bones run."

Jerome, who had been standing out of the way, now stepped forward. "Tree Tall rides like he was born to it. The soldiers at the reservation all say so. Don't they, Matt?"

The red-haired Matt only smiled.

Glancing at his watch, the settler noted, "We've got an hour before race time. I'd better get these animals out there while everybody is here, to see if I can find a buyer." He started to lead the geldings away, calling back, "See you later, Tree Tall. And may the best horse and man win out there today."

The Indian boy thought he might be able to like the thickset settler. The man who had been treated unfairly by the soldiers had just called Tree Tall a man!

Deke walked up. He and Matt went into the stable to get Crow ready. Jerome motioned for Tree Tall to come with him and together they raced off toward the store. "My father said he'd let us have the leather. Your father was at the store. He was starting to cut out a loincloth for you when I left."

"It will be good to wear again," the Indian boy said.

They ran along the street, dodging people and horses. Right in front of the store Tree Tall noticed the biggest, tallest man he had ever seen. He was taller than anyone else who stood nearby. And he was big—not puffy fat like the settler, but big in the bones. And yet it was his hair that caught the boy's attention. It was white like snow. It grew down along his jaws fanning back over his ears like wings. Tree Tall stopped, staring at the big white-haired man.

Jerome stopped too. He nudged Tree .Tall. "That's Dr. John McLoughlin. The Indians call him Eagle because of his hair. He used to be head man at Fort Vancouver to the north. But now he lives here."

Jerome laughed. "Tree Tall! Close your mouth."

# 6

# Get Ready—Get Set

TREE TALL could feel the man's eyes turn toward him. "Good afternoon, boys. Planning to watch the race?"

"Yes, sir. I am at least," Jerome said. "Tree Tall here is riding in it."

"You don't say. That's a man-sized undertaking."

In that instant Tree Tall added another white man to his list of likes. Dr. McLoughlin thought of him as a man.

"Where do you live?" the white-haired McLoughlin asked Tree Tall. "I don't believe I've seen you before."

"Tree Tall live on reservation now."

"I see...." His voice trailed off. "I don't imagine it's easy for you there. Try to make the best of it, young man, and you'll do just fine."

74

"Come on," Jerome urged the Indian boy. "We've got to hurry."

Tree Tall nodded and started to follow Jerome into the store. The man turned to watch the two boys, calling after them. "Good luck, Tree Tall. You be careful out there today."

In the back room Tree Tall pulled his clothes off and put on the loincloth Gray Seal had made for him. His father watched with approval. It seemed good and right wearing it again. The boy could see an advantage in wearing the clothes of the whites now. They were warmer when the days and nights were cool, and much more comfortable than the scratchy bark material from which his people had made their coverings. But during the times of the warm days of sun, it was much better to wear only the loincloth, he decided.

Gray Seal looked at his son with longing in his eyes. "Tree Tall is now Indian again."

The boy knew his father wished to live and dress as they had before the white men came to their land. And yet, he had to admit there were some things that were better now. Was he not about to win a horse for himself? A horse would give him and his father social standing on the reservation with the other Indians. No one there, except the soldiers, had horses.

Tree Tall looked into his father's dark brooding face. "We will soon have the horse. Things

75

will be better for Gray Seal's family."

The man nodded. He reached out, gripping his son's shoulder. Speaking then with their own words, he said, "Tree Tall is almost a man. Maybe soon Gray Seal will give a rainy day festival to let the boy tell of his guardian spirit. Will give presents to all who come. Gray Seal will make many wood carvings. Trade much to the white store-man. Will give white man's trade things as gifts then to our people. This will show to others Gray Seal and Tree Tall are proud Indians again."

The boy felt happy inside. But he did not smile. What his father had said was a serious matter. An Indian's wealth and standing among his own people was proven by how many gifts he had to give away at festival times and at potlatches. Some would give nearly all they had. In return they would be invited to other gatherings. There they would receive back what they had given as well as additional gifts. This had long been the custom of their people.

"Come," Gray Seal said. "We must get Little Pine and Bright Sky. They will want to watch Tree Tall win the horse."

Jerome said he would wait at the store with his father. There were many people in town and his father needed help.

Tree Tall and Gray Seal went out onto the street alone, his father using the forked pole to help him walk. It suddenly dawned on the boy this was the first time they had walked among the whites of the town without being with Jerome or some member of his family. The people stared at the two Indians, especially at the boy wearing only the loincloth of elk hide.

A woman in a long-flowing dress stopped suddenly in front of Tree Tall, causing him to have to walk around her. She clucked her tongue in her mouth. Several others pointed at Tree Tall and laughed.

"What are those Indians doing here?" a man growled as Gray Seal and Tree Tall brushed past him. "Hey, someone find one of those soldiers. Have these Indians hauled back to the reservation."

"Yeah," another agreed. "They don't belong here."

"Come," Gray Seal spoke to Tree Tall as he hobbled along faster. "White people forget very fast. They are the ones who do not belong." He turned to Tree Tall. "Walk with head high."

Tree Tall was feeling shame—shame of his body covered only with the loincloth. But he kept his head high as his father had said to do. Together they broke out of the crowd in front of the store and continued on toward Jerome's house. No one attempted to stop them.

When they reached the tent they found Little Pine seated on the ground outside. She looked up as they approached. Bright Sky came out of the tent wearing a violet-colored dress Jerome's sister had given her, one the white girl had outgrown.

Surprised to see her son wearing the loincloth, Little Pine said, "This looks like the son I knew when he was a small boy in our old village—the boy who used to help me pick the blackberries. But what will the whiteskins say?"

Gray Seal told her of Jerome's idea. He explained how it would be better for Tree Tall to ride Crow without the pant legs of the whiteskin's clothes getting in his way.

"Horses will run very fast," Little Pine noted. "If Tree Tall falls he will be hurt, maybe like his father. Little Pine does not like this race!"

Bright Sky had been staring at Tree Tall. "Think Indian boy looks better in clothes of the whites."

"You will come watch the race?" Tree Tall asked his mother, ignoring the girl.

"Little Pine will wait here. Will not go to see her son run over by the white men's horses."

"I will go watch," Bright Sky spoke again. "Will then run back to tell Little Pine what happened."

Gray Seal and the two children walked to the stable. But instead of going on the street, they went along the back of the buildings until they reached the place where the horses were kept.

Deke and Matt were inside with Crow. The brown horse showed a spark of life in his eyes. He was not used to all the attention he had been receiving from his owner. The good grain, the rubdowns, and the special care were unusual.

Leaning on his pole, Gray Seal watched as Deke and Matt checked Crow's hooves and adjusted the bridle. The Indian man had never been in the shadowy stable with its musty smells. He looked down the line of the stalls at the horses stabled there. His eyes betrayed his longing to own such an animal.

Bright Sky pulled at Tree Tall's arm. He followed her off to the side, away from the others. "Bright Sky pray this morning for you and for Crow. Pray to your Great Spirit God and to Jesus. Does Tree Tall think God hears prayers of the girl?"

"Maybe," the boy replied. "Tree Tall has prayed, too."

"Hey," Matt was calling. "Why don't you show Gray Seal the mare we may win?"

The three Indians walked down the line of stalls until they came to a box stall where the bay mare was kept. Gray Seal looked at the mare over the top partition. "Look good," he commented. "Round belly show her young soon to be born."

"This foal may soon be Tree Tall and Gray Seal's horse," the boy reflected.

But inside he was wondering. He wanted the foal so much. He had prayed. And Bright Sky had prayed. He was certain Jesus knew his longing for a horse. But there were so many fast horses in the race today. And the path through the forest was full of trouble. Could he and Crow stay in front of the others so they could win this mare?

Fear twisted itself to a knot inside Tree Tall's stomach. He had not known such fear since he had been captured and chained by the white trappers near his old village. He had prayed then and the Great Spirit God had helped him get away. Would God help him win this horse race?

And if they did win, what about the settler? Tree Tall had seen fear in the boy Tom's eyes. He could tell the settler's son did not want to ride the stallion in this race. His father had lost horses to the Indians of the plains. He talked of debts, whatever that was. It seemed to have to do with the white man's money—something the man worried about. If Tree Tall won this race the settler would lose his mare and its soon-to-be-born foal, as well as the money he had put up for the race. The Indian boy remembered how the settler had called him a man that day. It saddened him just a little to think of the settler losing the race.

But still.... He would enjoy winning. It

would be a great triumph. Although he guessed most of Tom's bragging ways were to cover his fears, it would be good to cross the finish line ahead of the white boy and the stallion. It would be good to see the faces of the white people, too, who had laughed and pointed.

"Tree Tall." Matt was calling him.

The boy looked away from the mare.

"It's time to go," the red-haired soldier said.

Deke boosted Tree Tall up on Crow's narrow back, keeping the reins. He led the horse out of the dark stable and into the sun-warmed street. The other contestants were all there, walking or loping their horses back and forth, warming them up among the people who had come to watch the long-talked-of race.

Tree Tall sat proudly on Crow's back. He knew they must look strange—the ugly brown horse, with not even enough coloring to be called a bay, and the bare-bodied dark-skinned Indian boy, saddleless astride the big-boned animal. They made their way down the dusty street. Deke led Crow with Matt, Gray Seal, and Bright Sky following. Tree Tall looked at the other horses. Tom was there on the black. The sight of the stallion sent a thrill through Tree Tall. Would the foal of the bay mare look anything like this stallion when it was grown?

They were drawing near Jerome's father's store and the starting line. Tree Tall saw the tall white-haired man called McLoughlin. The man's light-colored eyes were looking his way. He raised a hand in a sort of salute, much the way Tree Tall had seen soldiers greet one another. Tree Tall lifted his own hand to return the salute. The big man smiled.

On the wooden platform in front of the store he could see Gray Seal and Bright Sky with Matt. His father stood tall and proud, the pole he used for walking placed against the store building behind him.

Jerome and his family were there, too. Jerome's father had just come out of the building and was locking the door behind him. It would not be unlocked again for business, Jerome had told Tree Tall, until after the race. Jerome did not wave, but Tree Tall knew his friend was with him in spirit this day. They were, after all, much like brothers. They had pledged to remain friends before Jerome had left the camp where his family lived for a time near Tree Tall's old village. That was before the soldiers had come to take the Indians to the reservation.

"All right, everyone. Clear the street! The race is about to start!" The words came from a man who stood high up on the only wagon left at the side of the street. The others had all been moved out of the way between buildings or around behind.

People hurried to find a place from which to

watch. Soon the center of the street was empty except for the ten horses and their riders and a few men who were helping. Deke pulled the reins up over Crow's head, handing them to Tree Tall while keeping hold of the bridle. Tree Tall sat straight on Crow's back as Deke led the horse toward the starting line. People were looking toward him and laughing. But Tree Tall knew they would soon see how fast Crow could run. They would not be laughing for long.

The man standing on the wagon was talking again. "You've all chosen numbers for your places in line. As I call out a name, line up side by side, beginning on the north side of the street."

A name was called. Then another. Two horses were moved to the starting line facing west. Tom's name was called next. The plump white boy coaxed the black stallion into place. His father moved to stand at the stallion's head, holding the spirited animal in check.

"Next," the man on the wagon was announcing, "we have Matthew Stone."

Tree Tall glanced at the man. It was strange hearing the name the soldiers had given him. But before it was only on paper that Tree Tall was called Matthew Stone. Never had anyone called him that until now. Not his family. Not Jerome. Not even Matt or Deke. He wanted to shout so everyone could hear, "My name is Tree

83

Tall!" But he did not. There were other more important things to think about now.

Deke positioned Crow into line beside Tom and the fidgety black. The portly settler appeared nervous. He wiped at the sweat beading on his forehead. Tree Tall turned to the sandy-haired boy beside him on the stallion. But Tom was looking straight ahead. The skin of his face had turned a sort of transparent white.

The man on the wagon was explaining the horse the Indian boy called Matthew Stone was riding. "This horse is owned by Deke Townsend, a soldier stationed on the reservation. He says he found the horse along the trail on their way west. He calls him Crow."

There was a ripple of laughter along the line of people on either side of the street. The man on the wagon continued. "This soldier fella claims Crow can run." Again there was laughter. "Guess we'll soon find out, folks."

# 7

# And They're Off!

THE SETTLER looked up at Tree Tall and then at Tom. His face stretched into a tight smile. "Do the best you can. Both of you." He spoke then only to Tom. "Remember, son, I'm counting on you. We've got a lot at risk here."

Tree Tall glanced at Tom. "Be careful of bad places on trail."

The white boy appeared not to hear.

The other horses and riders were called into line one by one. At last they were ready. The man on the wagon had a handgun like the soldiers carried. He held it high in the air, pointing the hollow end toward the sky.

Deke looked up at Tree Tall. "Kick Crow into action the minute that gun fires. Understand?"

Tree Tall nodded.

The settler, Deke, and the others who had

been helping with the horses moved away. At last there were only the ten horses and their riders lined-out across the wide street of dust. All became quiet. No one talked. Somewhere a baby cried out, then all was still again.

Ahead of them was the forest race course. It would be narrow there. Some horses would have to drop back or they would pile into one another. The first ones to turn off onto the trail would have the advantage.

Tree Tall gripped his legs tighter around Crow's middle. He pulled up slightly on the reins to let the horse know he was about to ask for action.

Just then a couple horses bolted from the starting line, only to be brought back to take their places again. Tree Tall heard Tom suck in a raw gasp of air as his own stomach did a flip-flop.

Then everything happened at once. The gun went off with a roar. All ten horses leaped ahead as one. The people watching yelled. And Crow, with Tree Tall atop, was in the very center of it all.

Crow seemed to explode under Tree Tall. The brown horse's head and body lined-out straight as he reached forward with a long ground-eating stride. He and the black stallion were in the lead. Tree Tall had no idea how far back the other riders were.

**Old Crow and the black horse were in the lead. Tree Tall
had no idea how far back the other riders were.**

The Indian boy leaned low over Crow's neck. His hands froze on the reins; his body stiffened. He had ridden Crow fast before, but never this fast. He felt numb. Could he stay on? They were nearing the end of the street. The forest path was just ahead, beyond the bend of the road. The boy pulled on the reins to slow the brown horse.

Tree Tall looked again toward the black. The stallion was inching ahead. Tree Tall had a quick glimpse of Tom's face. The white boy seemed in shock. Tree Tall pulled back again on the reins. This was too fast! Way too fast to make the turn onto the path.

A light cream horse started to pass Crow on the left. Tom was in front now. There was the trail. It was just ahead. The black and the cream turned onto it without losing a beat in their hard pumping strides. Tree Tall leaned his body in the direction of the trail as a bay horse crept up beside them. Crow swung hard onto the path, nearly unseating Tree Tall. Crow and the bay were now side by side. Tom and the black were ahead. The cream horse was in between. Somewhere behind came the pounding hooves of the other six. Tree Tall did not bother to look back.

The boy was sighting between Crow's ears. A man stood close to a slight rise in the trail ahead. Tree Tall remembered hearing there would be men called judges stationed along the course to make sure all went right.

The bay was easing ahead of Crow now. Tree Tall was fourth from the front. The thick fear that had deadened his mind and body began to clear. He still held a taut rein on Crow, not giving him freedom to run as the boy knew he could. It was not fair to the horse or to Deke. He would never win a horse of his own if he did not allow Crow to do what he could do best—run!

The four lead horses strung out along a narrow section of trail. They had passed the first judge and were starting up a steep hill. The bay just ahead seemed to slow. Tree Tall leaned to one side as he loosened his hold on the reins. Crow responded, crowding the bay to inch up beside him. Tree Tall heard the bay horse's rider curse. He did not look at the man. There was room here for two horses. The bay's rider was trying to keep Crow from passing by riding in the center of the trail. Crow leaned into the bay, moving him just enough to pass.

At the top of the hill was another judge. The man called out encouragingly as the horses thundered by. Galloping down the opposite side was more difficult. Tree Tall hung onto Crow's wispy mane to keep from going over the brown horse's head. The cream and the black were still holding their places ahead of him. At the bottom of the hill the trail turned hard to the north. Crow took the turn without a break in stride.

Tree Tall felt Crow's front legs change leads with an effortless move, reaching out first with the left leg rather than the right to keep from being thrown off balance.

Another judge watched from back off the trail. "Hang in there, fellas!" the man called after them. There were switchbacks just ahead. Tree Tall took a tighter grip on the reins to slow Crow enough to keep to the trail. But before he could put pressure on them, Crow braced himself for the tight turns. It was then the boy gave up trying to show Crow anything. He just hung on. The old horse had probably been in more races than Tree Tall would ever see.

With the switchbacks behind, Tree Tall looked up at Tom and the black again. They were not any further ahead, just keeping the same distance between them as they had when they first left the road for the forest trail. The cream in between Crow and the stallion was hanging in there, too.

They charged past another judge at a shallow creek. Crow leaped the narrow waterway, nearly unseating his rider again. It was all the boy could do to stay on the brown horse. He began wishing he had learned to ride with a saddle.

A level section of the trail lay just ahead. Tree Tall saw two more judges there. The trail widened then. Before he could decide what to do, Crow was running eye-to-stirrup with the rider

90

of the cream horse. Tree Tall was by now simply a passenger on the brown horse's back.

When they reached the next curve Crow was side by side with the cream. "Come on!" Tree Tall yelled in the horse's ears. "Run! Run! Run!" Crow bounded ahead.

They were over halfway around the course now. Halfway and there was only one horse— the black stallion—ahead of them. Only one horse to keep Tree Tall from winning the bay mare and her foal.

More tight turns slowed Crow's stride. The horse seemed to remember them as well as his rider. Tree Tall felt the brown horse tense, shifting his weight to his hind quarters to lean into the first turn. Tree Tall glanced up. Crow's nose was at the black's flank. Tom looked back. Surprise flashed across the white boy's round face.

Digging his heels into the stallion's sides, Tom urged his horse ahead again. But Crow was not to be left behind. The old horse Tree Tall had once called ugly, became a thing of beauty as he ran. The boy could feel it under him. He could feel Crow's muscles, legs, and heart working as one.

Around another turn and Crow was again sending his warm breath against Tom's leg. But the trail here was too narrow to pass. They thundered by another judge. Tree Tall glanced back. All he could see was the cream and the

91

bay. The others were still behind somewhere, out of sight around the last bend of the trail. Another turn brought them to a wide section again. Tree Tall pressed his hands hard against Crow's thin neck.

The brown horse responded, leaping ahead with another burst of speed. He and Tom were leg to leg now. But Tree Tall did not look at the white boy. He was staring straight ahead. There was nothing in front of them now but the empty trail. They would soon come onto the road that led back to Oregon City. If he could just get in front of the black and stay there, he would win the race and the mare.

Tree Tall heard a yell. It came from beside him. Tom shouted again, and the black leaped ahead. Crow was once more behind, his head at the stallion's flank. The trail remained wide here, except for one last narrow turn at the crest of a slight hill. Tree Tall looked for a judge. But no one was there. He urged Crow faster. The brown horse was struggling ... trying ... but could not find the strength to pass the black again. Glancing back Tree Tall saw they were leaving the others farther and farther behind.

They were nearly to the curve. Tree Tall wanted to get around the black before they came out of the turn. But Crow just did not have it in him. The brown horse was breathing hard. His gait had changed. It was uneven and choppy.

The stallion was tiring too. As they started into the curve the black faltered. His rhythmic stride broke as he tried shifting leads with his front legs. Crow was laboring too, seeming content to keep his nose a foot or so behind the black.

Then it happened.... It was like a dream. Tree Tall saw it all slowly moving before his eyes in pictures that seemed unreal. The black was going down. Falling.... His head was out of sight. His rump and hind legs were in the air. Crow swung hard to the side, easing past the falling horse. Tree Tall looked to the right in time to see Tom fly through the air over the stallion's head. He heard the black crash to the ground just as Tom was thrown against a tree with a sickening thud, falling face down onto the soft earth.

Crow seemed to gain strength now that he was in the lead. Tree Tall felt the brown horse surge to life under him again. The mare and the money for Deke, the foal for him, it would soon all be theirs. Tree Tall glanced back. Tom lay on the ground under the tree. He had not moved. The black was back on its feet galloping loose off the trail into the brush. The bay and the cream horses were coming up fast, passing the place where Tom lay. The white men looked at the boy lying so still beside the trail, but they did not stop to help or to see if Tom was alive.

Then, as a part of this awful dream—a dream from which Tree Tall could not escape—Jerome's words came to him: "Jesus said we are to love our neighbor as we love ourselves." Jerome's father's words rang in Tree Tall's thinking too. "It would be like you finding a white man and helping him. . . ."

Crow had reached the end of the forest trail. A turn to the west would take them straight onto the Oregon City street and the finish line where the people waited. But Tree Tall knew what he had to do. He would think about it for many days, even for years after this moment. But right now he knew what had to be done.

Pulling hard on the reins, the Indian boy slowed the brown horse enough to turn him into some brush alongside the road. Crow slid to a stop, burying his head among the scrub branches as the cream horse hurled on past. Next came the bay.

Tree Tall pulled Crow around and started back to where Tom lay. The other horses were coming hard toward them. The riders glanced down at the white boy as they passed, but no one stopped. There was room on the trail here for them to pass Crow as he backtracked the trail at a lope.

Tree Tall pulled the hard-breathing horse to a stop by the motionless form of the white boy and slipped from Crow's wet steaming back.

"Tom?" Tree Tall called softly as he bent over the boy. "Tom?"

The white boy lay crumpled in a heap at the base of the tree he had been thrown against when the stallion went down. He lay half-doubled over, his face buried in the moist earth beneath the tree. There was blood. It came from a wide gash on Tom's upper arm.

"Tom!" Tree Tall called again, turning the boy's face so his nose and mouth were out of the dirt so he could breathe. Had Tom's face been buried in the dirt too long, robbing him of air? Tree Tall touched Tom's round cheek. Was he dead? Fear stabbed at the Indian boy. He wanted to run from there as fast as he could. The blood! There was so much—too much— coming from the arm wound.

Tree Tall glanced at Crow. The horse stood where he had left him, his head nearly to the ground, his body swaying with each raw raspy breath. Although Tree Tall knew it to be wrong to even think at this moment, he could not help wondering if he had forfeited a race Crow would have won just to help a boy already dead. It did not seem fair when there had been so much at stake.

The Indian boy shook the thoughts away. "Must help Tom," Tree Tall declared aloud. But how? He knew he would have to stop the flow of blood or else the boy would soon die . . . if he was not already dead. But Tree Tall had nothing to use. He looked around. Moss grew on the side of the tree. He jumped up to pull off a handful as high as he could reach. With this he bent back to the boy, pressing the wad against the wound. The moss turned a bright soggy red. It was not helping.

The first panic that had swept over Tree Tall rolled away now as he turned to the only source of help he had. The race had been lost. There was no use thinking of that any longer. "Jesus," he prayed aloud. "Help Tree Tall to know what to do for Tom. Please. . . ."

Just then he noticed that the boy's shirt sleeve had nearly been torn off. Shreds of cloth hung from a shoulder seam. Tree Tall grasped the cloth and pulled it free. Slipping it under the boy's limp arm, he knotted it tight above the bleeding wound. The blood still ran fast from the wide cut. Tree Tall pulled the cloth tighter. At last the flow of red slowed. It was working! "Thank you, Jesus," the Indian boy whispered.

Tom's hand moved. Tree Tall looked again at the boy's white face. His eyes were open. He was staring up at the Indian boy. Tree Tall sighed with relief. Tom was not dead. "You hurt bad. Must lay still."

"Where is—is the stallion?" Tom asked, his voice weak and low.

Tree Tall glanced around. "Run off in brush."

"He didn't break a leg then?" Tom questioned.

"Run away on four legs. Maybe is hurt some, but not like boy."

Moving around to look at his arm, the one Tree Tall was holding the cloth around, Tom asked, "What are you doing?"

"Keep blood from running all out."

"My arm throbs. Can't you loosen up a little?"

Tree Tall let go of the cloth. But the blood gushed again from the open wound. Quickly he tightened it. "Keep tight. Much blood run out."

It was then he heard horses. They were coming fast. He glanced down the trail. The settler, Tom's father, and some others were galloping toward them. Behind he saw a wagon pulled by two horses bouncing along the trail, coming their way. "Father come now. Bring help."

The horses slid to a stop beside Crow. "What happened here?" the settler shouted as he swung down from his horse. The stout man brushed past Tree Tall, pushing him aside. "Tom! Are you all right?"

"I don't think so," the white boy replied weakly.

Tree Tall stood there not knowing what to do. The settler glared at the Indian boy as he bent over his son. "What have you done to Tom? What's this around his arm?"

# 8

# His Head High

AS THE MAN loosened the cloth, blood again gushed from Tom's arm. "Not take off!" the Indian boy spoke. "Blood will all run out."

The wagon reached them then and a man climbed down carrying a black bag. "Doc," the settler pleaded, "help Tom. Please."

Tree Tall stepped back as the man with the black bag bent over the white boy. He tightened the cloth around Tom's arm again and the bleeding slowed. "Let's get him in the wagon and back to my office," the doctor said.

Tree Tall was pushed out of the way as the other men, who had ridden out with the settler from town, lifted Tom into the wagon. The Indian boy stepped back to stand by Crow. This was not the big whitehaired Dr. McLoughlin Tree Tall had met before the race.

As the team was backed up to turn the wagon around, the settler stopped in front of the boy. "Where's my stallion?"

"Run off in brush."

The stout man stood looking at the Indian for a few seconds. "What happened out here? The other riders said the last they saw of you and Tom, before they found Tom lying here and you headed back toward him, the stallion was in the lead and you were right on his tail trying to pass. What did you do?"

Shaking his head Tree Tall answered, "Do nothing. Crow and stallion get very tired. Stallion fall."

"You made him fall!" The man's face was turning a bright pink. "Your friends, the soldiers, took my rider out of the race. Then you bring my stallion down," he said, his voice edged with rage.

"No!" Tree Tall declared. "Tree Tall come back. Others all go on by. No one help Tom."

"You were scared." The man turned to mount his horse. "That's what happened, all right. You got scared and came back to cover up whatever it was you did. Why else would you forfeit the race!"

Tree Tall stared up as the man pulled his horse around. Then the settler and the others rode off to follow the wagon back to town. Tree Tall wanted to cry. He wanted to lay down flat

"You were right on his tail trying to pass. What did you do?"
the man shouted. "You made him fall!"

on the ground and cry until no more tears would come. But he was too old to cry. Only the Indian woman and the girl cried. Not men. He wondered why. It would be good to let out the hurt that was burning his insides.

He had lost the race. Deke had lost the money he had paid to enter the race as well as the prize money and the mare he would have won if Tree Tall had not stopped to help Tom. Tree Tall would not get the foal. The soldiers who had bet their money would lose it. The work of Matt, Deke, and Crow to get ready for the race, had all been for nothing.

His father had counted on the horse Tree Tall would have won, to give them standing among their own people. Now that could not be. The settler's people who had laughed at Crow and Tree Tall would be angry with him, like the settler, thinking he had done something to Tom and the stallion to keep them from winning.

Tom would have won the race if the black had not fallen. At the least it appeared he would have. Crow had given all he had, more than the other horses in the race, but the black was not like the others. Crow was not as fast or as young as the stallion.

Yes, Tree Tall thought to himself, it would be good to lay down on the warm moist earth and cry. But he could not. He would not!

He looked at Crow. The horse was breathing

easier now. If there had been a saddle on the brown horse Tree Tall could get back on. But there was no saddle, and Crow was too tall for him to mount bareback without help.

The boy pulled the reins down over Crow's head and started walking—leading the horse toward the white man's town. If he could just get onto Crow maybe he would be able to find the stallion. That might make the settler feel a little better toward him.

When the boy and the brown horse reached the main road, Tree Tall saw Matt and Deke riding their way. "What happened out here?" Matt called, pulling Red to a stop.

Deke was right behind him. "They told us you made the stallion fall. Is that right?"

"Tree Tall do nothing. Only help the boy Tom."

"Are you all right?" Matt questioned.

The Indian boy nodded.

Matt stepped down from Red to boost Tree Tall on Crow's back. "So what happened?" Matt asked again.

Tree Tall told them then, glancing at Deke from time to time. Deke sat on his horse glaring at him, not saying a word. When Tree Tall finished, Deke said, "What it amounts to is you lost the race when you could have won!"

Looking down, away from the accusing eyes of the white soldier, Tree Tall sighed. It was true. He nodded. "Tree Tall lose race. Lose money and horse for Deke. Lose foal for Tree Tall. . . ."

Matt rode beside the boy on the way back to town. Deke, however, galloped on ahead, turning to shout back, "Have your family ready to leave just as soon as I get the wagon hitched. Understand?"

Tree Tall understood. They would have to leave the white man's town very fast.

Matt said nothing on the ride back to town. Was he angry too?

When they reached the street it was once again filled with people, horses, and wagons. And, once again, Tree Tall felt naked wearing only the loincloth. The wagon that had brought Tom back was standing empty outside a building. Tom and his father were nowhere in sight. Tree Tall glanced at the people to see if the big white-haired McLoughlin was among them. He was not.

Matt stopped his horse in front of the store of Jerome's father. Tree Tall saw Little Pine, Gray Seal, and Bright Sky standing there. Jerome and his mother and sister were there, too. The door to the store was open again and people were going and coming.

Little Pine started toward her son as he pulled to a stop beside Matt. But Gray Seal stopped her. Was his father angry too? His mother spoke to him. "Are you all right?" she asked using their Indian words.

The boy nodded.

Several soldiers came toward them from across the street. One yanked Tree Tall off Crow's back. "You rotten Indian. You're to blame for us losing our money!"

Gray Seal moved toward the soldier as Jerome's father came to the open door. "Wait just a minute, there," the store-man spoke. "That boy did not talk you into betting your money. That was your decision. So leave him be."

Deke was walking toward them now. "That's right. I tried warning you. I tried tellin' you how fast I thought that black was. But not a one of you would listen."

The soldier turned on Deke as though to strike him. "You and that mangy brown horse ought to be whipped. You're always braggin' how fast he is. It's your fault as much as it is this kid's."

"Tree Tall," Jerome's father said. "Come into the store."

Matt spoke up. "We've got to head out of here right away. Tree Tall and his family had better go back to your place to pack their things."

"Give us just a few minutes," the store-man said. "I want to talk to the boy."

"Okay. . . ." Matt looked at Gray Seal and Little Pine. "You'd better come with me. I'll help take the tent down while Deke goes after the team and wagon."

Tree Tall went into the store following Jerome's father to the back room. Jerome and Bright Sky tagged along. The man closed the door behind the three children then shoved a box toward the Indian boy. "Sit down. You look exhausted. Tell us what happened out there on the trail."

Tree Tall took a deep breath and again told the story of the black's fall and how he had turned back to help Tom. He told how the words of Jerome and his father had come to him, of how the story from the Bible book had spoke to his heart.

"What you did was right," the man told him. "You would probably have won the race if you had not stopped. But it's doubtful they would have given you the prize money and the mare. There would still have been the claim you caused the accident to keep young Tom from winning."

"Tree Tall not cause!" the boy asserted again.

"I believe you. I'm just telling you what the others would have said."

"Settler already say this to Tree Tall."

"He may see things differently after his boy is better. If Tom recovers. Then again, Tom may let his father think you caused his horse to go down. Or he may even believe you did."

Jerome spoke up then. "Can't we do something to help?"

The man was shaking his head. "I don't know of a thing that would help right now. We can pray. And we will. But nothing else is going to help at this moment."

The Indian girl poked at Tree Tall. "Must go now. Hurry, like Matt said."

"That's probably best," Jerome's father agreed. "Let things cool down around here."

Tree Tall stood up, starting toward the front of the store with his head down. He did not want to have to look into the faces of the white people out there.

"Tree Tall," the man called to him.

The boy stopped, looking back at the man. "You hold your head high. Remember, God honors those who love him, those who love others as themselves. Before Jesus left this earth he said he would never leave us or forsake—that means forget—us. Whatever happens now, you keep your mind on that. Jesus cares. He'll take care of you. You honored him today by loving your fellowman when you went back to help Tom, just like the story Jesus told about the good Samaritan. I believe God will honor you somehow for what you did today."

The Indian boy looked at the white man. "Tree Tall will try to think on this."

The man picked up the clothes the boy had

106

taken off before the race so he could wear the loincloth his father had made. "You'd better put these on before you go out there again."

Tree Tall nodded, glancing at Bright Sky. The girl turned and went out to the front of the store while he changed back into the white man's clothes. Then he and Jerome walked out onto the street with Bright Sky. They could see Matt with the wagon in front of Jerome's house. Deke was there on his horse, too, holding the lead ropes to Red and Crow. People standing in front of the store looked at the Indian youngsters and pulled away.

And then, from across the street, the settler came out of a building and climbed up to stand in the wagon they had used to bring Tom back to town. "Listen, everyone," he called, motioning the people to gather around.

Those in the street wandered over toward the wagon.

"The doc says Tom will be all right in time. He's lost a lot of blood, but there's no broken bones."

The people kind of sighed all at the same time. Tree Tall stood away from them there in the center of the street. He was glad Tom would be all right. The white boy might have been dead by now if he had not gone back to stop the blood from all running out on the ground. The white people did not know this. But he knew he had done what was right. Jerome's father said Jesus knew, too. It would help, though, if these white people could know.

Jerome prodded him to hurry along. But the settler was talking again. "I said I would give the mare to the winner of the race. And there's the fifty dollars I put up as well as the money the other contestants paid to enter. I don't think I need to tell any of you I sure did not expect my stallion to lose. And I'm sure he wouldn't have if. . . ." The plump man stopped and looked toward Tree Tall.

"Come on," Bright Sky whispered. "People get madder soon. We hurry now."

But the Indian boy was shaking his head. He pointed toward the stable. Someone was leading the bay mare toward them. The settler looked at the faces in the crowd below him. "Charlie Green? Are you here?"

A man, the one Tree Tall recognized as the rider of the cream horse, stepped onto the wagon beside the settler. The man called Charlie was smiling. Tree Tall wondered if Charlie felt at all bad about not stopping to help the settler's son.

Tom's father was talking again. "Charlie, here's the money you won. And there's the mare." With that the settler smiled and shook the man Charlie's hand. But the smile was weak and the handshake brief.

Tree Tall turned away. He walked with Jerome and Bright Sky in silence back to Jerome's house where his father and mother waited in the wagon with Matt. He wondered about the settler. The man had told Matt he needed to sell a horse because he had to get some money. That was probably why he had offered to race his stallion. He figured if the black won, and he certainly would have, he would get all his money back, keep his mare, and win the money the other contestants had paid to enter the race. Now his son was hurt and he had lost all he had offered. Even though the settler and his son had not treated Tree Tall well, the boy could not help feeling sorry for them too. He comforted himself with the fact that at least Tom was alive. Maybe the others thought the accident was Tree Tall's fault. But he knew it was not. And Jesus knew.

When the children reached the wagon they saw the stallion being led back to town by a couple riders. Sweat was dried on the black's coat, but he was alert, trotting with a spring to his gait, his ears pointed forward and his head high. Tree Tall was glad the stallion was not hurt.

There was time only for a quick good-bye to Jerome and his sister before Matt started the wagon moving. Tree Tall pushed Bright Sky up over the backtailgate then jumped on after her.

Deke kicked his horse into a lope, riding off ahead leading Red and Crow. Gray Seal was not sitting on the high seat with Matt this time. Instead he sat in back with his family. Matt made a wide turn heading back toward the center of town. They would have to go right through the middle of the crowd.

Matt slapped the team into a brisk trot.

# 9

# Condemned

"THERE GO those redskins!" someone yelled from the crowd.

"Good riddance!" called out another. "We can do without their kind."

Tree Tall's eyes sought those of his mother and father. But Little Pine, her back against the high front seat, kept her head down. Gray Seal sat at one side, an arm resting on the top edge of the wagon box. His head was high but his eyes stared off at nothing.

At last they rounded the bend. The town was behind them. The Indian family rode in silence for a long time. Matt was quiet, too.

At last Gray Seal looked at his son. Speaking with the words of their people, he said, "Gray Seal does not believe Tree Tall hurt the white boy or made the horse fall."

111

Tree Tall's heart skipped. "Gray Seal is wise," said the boy. He glanced then at his mother.

She was looking at them, smiling. "Gray Seal is a very understanding man. Very good man. The son is much like the father. Little Pine feels much pride."

Bright Sky touched the boy's arm. "The Indian boy did right."

Tree Tall let out a relieved sigh, looking at each family member. "Feel much better now."

Matt turned to look back at them as he drove the team. "What did they say?" he asked.

The boy related his parents' words.

"It's not going to be easy for any of you when we get back to the reservation," Matt reminded them. "Not when the soldiers who lost their money on the race return."

Farther up the road they met Deke. He waited on his horse, holding the ropes to Red and Crow. Matt stopped the wagon and Deke tied the two extra horses to the back. Then they started off again at a quick trot with Deke riding out in front. Tree Tall felt sorry for Crow. The old horse was tired. He needed rest, not a long journey yet that day.

It was late when they stopped for the night. Tree Tall wanted to help care for Crow, but Deke would not allow him near the brown horse. The next day they were on the trail again early. Three days passed.

The morning of their last day of travel the captain and his men caught up with them. Tree Tall could not tell how the captain felt. But the others were loud with their anger.

Words were hurled at Tree Tall as the soldiers followed the wagon, riding in a half circle at the back. "There's that rotten Indian kid," one said.

"Hey, there, Indian boy, lost any good races lately?" another called.

"I've a mind to make you crawl back to the reservation for what you did to us," said another.

The boy glanced at Gray Seal. His father's eyes were sullen. His mother again had her head down. Bright Sky crept behind Little Pine.

At last the captain made the others stop hurling their insults at the boy. "That's enough! It's over and done. Leave the boy alone."

"But, Captain . . ." a man started to protest.

"It's enough!" the captain ordered.

"Captain, sir," a tall mustached man spoke as he gave a stiff salute. "I think we'd all feel better if we could punish the boy some. I know I would."

The captain, who rode his horse with his back straight as a rod, asked, "Such as?"

"I'd like to see him down on the ground walking. How about the rest of you?"

"Yeah," the others intoned.

They rode on for a few minutes. At last the

captain ordered the wagon stopped. His eyes were on Tree Tall. "I think it would be best if you got down and walked, Matthew."

There was that white man's name again. Tree Tall sat there just looking at the captain. Gray Seal moved to protect his son as the tall mustached one nudged his horse up against the wagon. The soldier grabbed Tree Tall by the arm as Gray Seal stood up, bringing his walking pole down hard across the white man's shoulders. But the soldier kept his hold on the boy, pulling him to the ground. Tree Tall fell in a heap between Red and Crow. The two horses shied, fanning apart to step away from the boy.

"That's enough," the captain cautioned. "Get up, Matthew." He looked up at Matt on the high wagon seat. "Start the team," he said.

The wagon began to move. Tree Tall scrambled to his feet. He did not wish to be left behind alone with the soldiers. He had to walk fast to keep up. But he was strong. It would not hurt him to walk. The soldiers fell back to bring up the rear. Finally they let up their laughing and jeering, calling the boy names he had never before heard.

After a time Bright Sky jumped down to walk with Tree Tall. He glanced at her and smiled. "Hold your head high, Indian girl. Never let white soldiers see shame."

The girl nodded.

They walked in silence for a time, then Bright Sky asked, "Why did the Great Spirit God not hear the prayers of Tree Tall and Bright Sky? Why did not Tree Tall and Crow win the race?"

The boy thought for a time before answering. "Great God and Son Jesus did hear prayers, Tree Tall thinks. But maybe the others prayed, too."

His mind struggled with Bright Sky's question as they trudged behind the wagon in the dust raised by the turning wheels. He had also been wondering and questioning. At last he spoke again. "Many days back, when my people were first taken to the reservation, Tree Tall felt much anger at the Great Spirit God. It made hurt inside go deep. Tree Tall remembers now something Jerome told about Jesus, about how people treated God's Son when he walked the earth. Tree Tall knows now how Jesus felt when he was hated for doing right."

The boy smiled ever so slightly. "It makes the Indian boy feel very close to God. Tree Tall thinks he will be wise to keep Jesus as his guardian Spirit."

Bright Sky sighed. "Jerome's father said God would honor Tree Tall."

The boy shrugged. "Maybe. . . ."

As soon as the wagon reached the reservation, the mounted soldiers and their captain rode off. Deke untied Crow from the wagon without even a glance at Tree Tall or his family, leaving Matt to unload the Indian's things and unhitch the team alone. Matt had remained quiet during most of the trip. He had not been unkind, just not his usual friendly self.

As Tree Tall's family gathered their belongings to carry back to their lodge in the forest clearing, the boy went to where Matt was unhooking the horses from the wagon. "Is Matt angry with Tree Tall, too?"

The red-haired white man did not answer. Tree Tall waited. At last Matt slowly straightened, looking directly into Tree Tall's dark eyes. "I was. But I'm not any longer. You've got enough folks workin' their mad out on you. I guess I'd rather be your friend."

The boy smiled. "That is good." He turned to go help his family.

"But, Tree Tall," Matt called after him, "tell me just one thing. Why didn't you finish the race and then go back to see about Tom? You could have told us as soon as you crossed the finish line. We would all have gone back to help. Didn't you think of that?"

"Tree Tall see Tom's face in dirt. White boy lay very still. Tree Tall think then of Bible and Samaritan man."

Matt was staring at the boy. "You mean the Bible story about the good Samaritan?"

"Jerome's father read Bible book one night

about this man," Tree Tall explained.

Matt nodded. "I remember hearing that story when I was a kid on the farm."

The boy was tired from walking behind the wagon that day, but he followed his family without complaint to the clearing. At their lodge they found Many Songs sitting alone watching Spotted Elk and other men from their old village build lodges nearby. The old woman only glanced at her family as they approached. At last she turned her head, fixing her eyes on her grandson. "So? Does the Indian boy return wealthy? Where is the horse there was so much talk of winning?"

Little Pine stopped beside her mother. She placed a gentle hand on the older woman's thin shoulder. "We will speak of it later."

Many Songs nodded, muttering, "Young one not win race. Bring no horse back to Gray Seal's lodge. Spirits of Gray Seal's family all bad now. Need better spirits."

"Soon," Little Pine announced, changing the subject, "we will have a window in our lodge like the whites have in their houses. The white store-man's woman said she will ask him to bring Little Pine a window for the baskets she trades." She glanced at her mother. "You will like having a window in our lodge."

But Many Songs turned away without response.

117

The next morning Little Pine and Bright Sky went to the river to bring back water in their tight-woven baskets. But they soon returned with them empty. Bright Sky was crying and Little Pine looked frightened. She told them, "Soldiers keep us away from river. Say if we want water, must send Tree Tall or a man to carry it."

Gray Seal was carving a wooden bowl. He shook his head. "It is not the work of the man to carry water."

"I know," Little Pine agreed. "But there is no other way."

"I will get water," Tree Tall declared from where he had been watching Gray Seal carve the wood. The boy took his mother's basket as well as Bright Sky's. "Soldiers still want to make Tree Tall small, like stubby bush instead of tall tree. But Tree Tall will not hang the head for doing what was right."

As he walked toward the forest trail that led to the main encampment by the river, Bright Sky ran to catch him. "I will come carry my basket back after it is filled," she offered.

Tree Tall nodded, walking in silence. He was not looking forward to being taunted by the soldiers again. But he could not allow his mother or Bright Sky to pay for what he had done. The other Indians in the big camp watched as Tree Tall made his way to the riverbank. Word had spread quickly about the Oregon City race.

At the river he found four white soldiers sitting on the rocks close to where people dipped their baskets into the water. "Well, look who's coming," one of them remarked as Tree Tall headed down to the water's edge. Bright Sky waited at the crest of the sloped bank.

"Say, it's that loser boy, isn't it," another jeered.

The others laughed.

Tree Tall bent to dip the first basket into the water as one of the soldiers picked up a large rock. The boy could see him out of the corner of his eye. He continued his errand without a hint of fear. But inside his heart had quickened its beat.

*Splash!*

The rock hit the water flat, right in front of the boy, sending a shower of droplets over him. He wiped his face with an arm, then bent to fill the second basket. As he turned to start up the bank where Bright Sky waited, two soldiers moved to stand in his way. Tree Tall stopped, looking into their faces.

One leaned forward to peer in the baskets. "Say, you've got some dirt in there, boy. Don't you think your mama would like clean water?" He reached out, dumping the contents of both baskets on the ground. Then he pushed Tree Tall back to the water's edge. "Now that you're an Indian girl, you'd better be learnin' how to carry water."

Anger and hurt flooded the boy. Why was he being punished for doing what was right and good? It was not fair. But he could not fight all these soldiers. It would do no good. In fact, it was probably what they wanted. If they found he would not back down, and yet could not be forced to fight, maybe they would tire of their sport and leave him alone.

He filled the baskets again. And again the soldier dumped out the water. Tree Tall filled the baskets a third time. He looked up at the two who stood in his way. "Little Pine, Tree Tall's mother, needs water."

"Yeah," the one said to the other. "That's enough for this time. Let him go."

Tree Tall struggled under the weight of both baskets until he reached the forest path. There he gave one to Bright Sky. He looked at his adopted sister. "You cry again?"

"Soldiers very bad!" she said with a sob.

"They are still angry."

She started to follow with her water basket, then stopped. "Tree Tall?"

The boy turned.

"Girls need guardian spirits, too. Bright Sky is soon old enough to find a spirit of her own. Will Gray Seal allow this?"

120

He shrugged, putting his basket down to rest.

She spoke again. "You did not go out and fast as Indian boys and girls have always done to find their guardian spirits."

"Did not need to go off alone to seek the spirit. Tree Tall asked Jesus to be his guardian. God's Spirit then came to Tree Tall. He lives now with the Indian boy."

"Could a girl do that, too?" she asked. "Could Bright Sky ask this Jesus to be her guardian Spirit? I mean, without staying days and nights alone in the forest with no food?"

"Yes," he answered. "But you want to do this after the trouble Tree Tall gets himself into by following the Spirit of this Jesus God?"

She looked at him long, her eyes seeming to take her far from that place where they stood. "Bright Sky see Tree Tall grow into man with Jesus God as his guardian Spirit. Tree Tall not cry like baby or run or fight. Tree Tall do what is good and right. Think Tree Tall could not do this without help of guardian Spirit. Bright Sky would like to have this same Spirit for her own."

# 10

# Thunder Hawk

TREE TALL picked up his water basket. "Come. We will talk again later."

It was quiet around the cooking fire in their lodge that morning. His family were all hurting inside. It made Tree Tall feel sad knowing what his decision to help Tom was doing to them.

A little later Matt rode his horse up to their lodge. He got off and bent to peer through the narrow doorway. He, too, was looking miserable. "I'm sorry about what happened at the river this morning," he spoke at last. "I just heard about it."

Tree Tall went outside with Matt, stopping beside Red to pet the friendly horse.

"You'd best not come to our part of camp for awhile," the young soldier said. "I'll bring Red here now and then for you to ride."

Tree Tall nodded. "Matt is good friend."

That evening Bright Sky and Tree Tall wandered off to explore the dense forest close to their lodge. Tree Tall missed not being around the soldiers' horses. He and the girl talked as they ducked under low branches searching out the underbrush for nothing in particular. She asked again about Jesus and he told her all that Jerome and his father had said about the Great Spirit God and his Son. He told how he had asked Jesus to come into his own life. At last Bright Sky asked if the boy would help her pray to the Great Spirit God.

They stood together under the thick branches of a fir tree and put their chins forward close to their chests, the way they had seen the white family do. Tree Tall had never before prayed when someone else was listening. He tried remembering the words he had said to the Great Spirit God when he became a Christ-follower. He spoke in his prayer of how Bright Sky wanted to be a follower of Jesus, too, so the Spirit God would come to live with her. The boy's words noted sorrow for both his and Bright Sky's bad ways, and how Bright Sky longed to be forgiven by Jesus.

He then helped Bright Sky pray the words, ending by telling her, "Now you must tell the Great God you are asking this because of all Jesus did for you when he died and then came back to life." He looked at the girl. "You know, Jesus lives forever now with all who believe in him."

The girl's eyes were wide when she looked up. She did then as he had told her to do. When she looked up again her eyes were shining. "It is strange. Bright Sky feels all light inside."

He nodded. "It is like all the inside hollow is filled with happiness when this Spirit comes."

Later, as they headed back through the heavy brush to their lodge, Tree Tall stopped. He thought he heard running water—the gurgling sound it makes as it ripples fast over rocks. He listened. Bright Sky heard it then, too. They began searching for the sound together. Then, by a large boulder at the base of a rocky hillside, they found water bubbling out of the earth. It ran downhill for about the length of a man's arm, then disappeared back into the ground.

"It is a spring that comes up out of the earth," Tree Tall exclaimed. "We can make a pool here. Will not have to get water from river now."

Bright Sky was excited. "It is because of the Great Spirit God, is it not? He is smiling on Tree Tall and Bright Sky this day."

The boy smiled. "Yes, he smiles, too."

For the next week Tree Tall endured the taunts of the soldiers. It was as he had thought, when he did not fight back or seem afraid, they at last left him alone. Still, he did not go to their camp or even to the encampment of the other Indians more than he had to. The Indian boys who belonged to the tribes of their former enemies—the ones who had troubled him when he first came to the reservation—were again calling him names. Tree Tall had helped the boys learn the white man's words and for a time they had left him alone. But now, since hearing about the race at Oregon City, the boys were again up to their old habits.

Tree Tall knew the school was nearly ready. The whites were putting up a building on a nearby hill. When the time of the long rains returned the children of the reservation would go there to learn the ways of the whites. Many Indians were moving away from the main encampment now, building their lodges here and there on the set-aside reservation land. Some Indian children would live too far away to come to the white man's school.

Bright Sky was looking forward to going there. Even Tree Tall had decided it would be good to learn the ways of the whites. If he had to live among them, he thought it would be wise to learn of their ways. He was glad their lodge was within walking distance of the school.

It was late afternoon one warm day when Tree Tall heard the sound of horse's hooves pounding on the forest trail that led back to the main encampment. He was outside carving a wooden cooking stick. Gray Seal had been watching, helping his son learn to use the knife. Tree Tall and Gray Seal now looked toward the forest path. Bright Sky and Little Pine, who had been cooking berries by an outside fire—berries they had gathered earlier—stopped their work. Many Songs was away somewhere as she usually was lately.

It was Matt. He galloped Red right up to their lodge, pulling the horse to a sliding stop. "Tree Tall! Come back to camp with me right away!"

The boy stood up. "What is wrong?"

"You've got to come right now," insisted Matt, looking at the others. "You'd all better come."

Bright Sky slipped behind Little Pine. Gray Seal slowly rose to his feet, reaching for his long forked pole. "Gray Seal will go with Tree Tall. Woman and girl will stay here."

"No." Matt was shaking his head. "They'd better come too."

Gray Seal appeared doubtful. But he had come to trust this white soldier with the red hair, and so at last he nodded. Together Tree Tall and his family followed behind Matt's horse to the camp of the soldiers. The boy's heart was pounding hard in his chest.

As they neared the camp they saw men on horses surrounded by soldiers who stood around them. Tree Tall remembered seeing some of the mounted men in Oregon City. The settler was there, too. Tree Tall walked slower as they neared the white men.

Matt pulled his horse to a stop, announcing, "Here he is."

The settler turned in the saddle. "Well, Tree Tall. . . ." The bulky-framed man maneuvered his horse so he was facing the Indian family. "I see your parents and sister are with you."

"Is. . . ? Is Tom. . . ?" Tree Tall tried, but he could not get all the words out. Maybe the white boy was still not well and his father had come to continue his anger.

The man nodded. "Tom's better."

"That is good," Tree Tall remarked.

"Tom told me what happened out on the trail. He's not sure why the stallion fell, but he said you had nothing to do with it. For a time things were not very clear in his mind. But as he recovered, it all came back to him."

The Indian boy said nothing. What was there to say to this man who talked with so many words?

"Charlie, the rider who crossed the finish line first," the settler continued, "came to see me the other day. He felt guilty for not stopping to help Tom the way you did. He told me Tom's face was buried in the dirt when he passed him. My son probably would have suffocated if you had not gone back when you did. The doc told me right off you had probably saved Tom's life by

127

puttin' the cloth around his arm to stop the bleeding. But I was too mad and upset about Tom bein' hurt, and losing my mare and money, to listen to him at the time."

Still the Indian boy did not respond. It was good to hear, but his mind would not let go of the humiliation he had carried for so many days.

The settler continued. "Anyway, I rode out here to tell you I'm sorry. And to thank you proper for saving Tom's life. You're a brave and thoughtful lad. One any man would be proud to have as a son, be he red or white."

Gray Seal stepped forward to stand beside Tree Tall. He put a hand on the boy's shoulder. "Gray Seal proud!"

The stout white man smiled. "And so you should be." He turned then and called to someone behind him. "Bring the gelding."

A man led a dusty-looking black horse through the circle of soldiers to where Tree Tall stood with Gray Seal. It was the two-year-old black with the brown-tipped nose and ears Tree Tall had seen in Oregon City—the one the settler had been trying to sell.

The man handed the black's lead rope to Tree Tall, then he stepped back. The boy took the rope, staring at the young gelding.

"He's yours, Tree Tall," the settler said. "I owe a lot of people a lot of money. I'll pay them all back in time. But I owe you more. I owe you for the life of my son. When the store owner told me of your longing for a horse, I decided this would be the best way to show my thanks."

"You give horse to Tree Tall?" the boy questioned in complete disbelief.

"That's what I'm doing. If you want him."

The boy nodded. "Tree Tall want horse very much!"

Matt, who still sat on Red, was grinning so wide his freckles stretched across his face in streaks. He looked around at the other soldiers. "Well? You got something to say to this boy now? Seems you've all had quite a bit to say to him the last couple weeks, none of it what I'd call good."

Two soldiers turned to wander away. Another kicked at a rock with his booted toe, but said nothing. At last a man complained, "We lost money on that race!"

"And just who told you to bet your money?" Matt reminded him.

The soldier who had spoken turned to follow the others toward the tents.

Just then Deke stepped away from the soldiers who remained. He came forward to where Tree Tall held the black gelding. "Well, I at least owe this boy an apology. We all do. He's been more of a man than any of us. Winnin' a horse race isn't important at all, compared to

"Winnin' a horse race isn't important at all, compared to savin' a life," Deke said. "Tree Tall, I'm sorry about the way I acted."

savin' a life. Tree Tall, I'm sorry about those things I said to you and the way I acted and all."

A couple others mumbled some words before walking away.

Matt laughed. "It's going to take some of 'em awhile to swallow their pride, Tree Tall. But I'd say you've won more than a horse race here to-day."

That night, back at their lodge, Matt helped Tree Tall and Gray Seal locate the best spot to stake the gelding out so he could graze. "He's a good-looking horse," Matt remarked. "Even with his brown nose and ears."

Tree Tall still could not believe this was his horse. The two-year-old had a shiny coat like the wings of the hawk that now glided above them. It was almost more than his heart could hold.

Bright Sky came near. "God of the Bible shows honor to boy. Like Jerome's father say."

"It seems so," Tree Tall agreed.

Gray Seal and Little Pine walked over to stand with Tree Tall. Many Songs had returned from wherever it was she always disappeared to. She came close. "Hear about horse," she said. "Hear of white man who says Tree Tall is brave. Many Songs tell other Indians she does not need white men to tell this of Tree Tall. A grandmother knows heart of a boy."

"What are you going to name your horse?" Matt asked.

Tree Tall looked up again at the hawk riding the wind channels of the darkening sky above. "Horse is dark, like the thunderclouds before lights flash from the sky. Shines like hawk's wings catch last of going-down-sun. Tree Tall will call him Thunder Hawk."

"Good name," Gray Seal asserted.

The others agreed, even his grandmother.

Tree Tall took his beaver sleeping robe out to stay beside Thunder Hawk that night. The young horse missed the horses he had been stabled with, calling out from time to time with a shrill whinny. The boy talked with soft-sounding words from where he lay and the horse at last came to him. Thunder Hawk's warm brown nose explored the boy's face, seeming to understand they now belonged to each other. Tree Tall was afraid to sleep for fear he would awake to find this had only been a dream and the dusty-black was not really his. But at last sleep came.

In the morning light Thunder Hawk was still there, his long legs folded under him lying on the ground beside the boy's beaver sleeping robe. Tree Tall awoke, but he did not move, watching the horse—his horse—as it lay close beside him.

Soon the long rains would return and he would spend most of the day at the white man's school. But until then he would work with Thunder Hawk. He and the horse would be good friends by the time school started.

Matt came every day to help Tree Tall with Thunder Hawk. Since there were no other horses close by, the blackish gelding turned to Tree Tall for companionship. Gray Seal, too, spent much time with them. Tree Tall told his father, "You will have to help look after Thunder Hawk during the days of the long rains when Tree Tall is at the white man's school."

The warm days grew shorter as damp mists drifted in from the wide saltwaters. Tree Tall realized how much he had to be thankful for. His family could now provide for their own needs since trading with Jerome's father. They had a new lodge with fresh water close by. He at last had a horse all his own. And now he and Bright Sky would soon go to school to learn about things they had never before imagined. And then, when the warm days of sun returned, Thunder Hawk would be old enough to ride.

Yes, he was truly happy. Jesus, his guardian Spirit, had kept his promise never to leave or forsake him. The Great Spirit God had indeed brought much honor to the Indian boy.

**Shirlee Evans** lives in the Pacific Northwest, where her mother's family came as settlers in 1846. It was such settlers who squeezed the Indians off their land. But Shirlee also possesses an Indian heritage from her father who is one eighth Cherokee.

Today she and her husband live on land shared by the beavers and other wild creatures near Battle Ground, Washington, about 30 miles southwest of Mount St. Helens. It was here they raised their two sons. As a grandmother of six now, Shirlee enjoys helping her husband, Bob, with his draft horse hobby and driving their team.

While raising their sons she free-lanced for Christian and horseman magazines, besides having a teen novel, *Robin and the Lovable Bronc*, published by Moody Press. After her sons were grown she went to work for a weekly newspaper, refining her writing and winning a state Sigma Delta Chi award for investigative reporting. Her education consists of high school plus a few college classes, along with a great deal of life experience.

Before leaving the newspaper she interviewed Bill Towner, a Siletz Indian of Oregon, who with others of his disbanded tribe was seeking reinstatement by the United States government. (This has since come to realization.) Towner's story of the hardships suffered by his people over 100 years before at the hands of white soldiers and settlers etched itself on Shirlee's heart. Had her pioneer ancestors taken part in those acts?

Then, in 1983, a camp director from Royal Ridges Retreat, a Christian organization where two of her grandchildren were enrolled in day camp, asked Shirlee to write an Indian adventure story for their use. And so the fictional tale of Tree Tall, complete with historic highlights, came to be written.

Shirlee was born near Centralia, Washington. She manages to write several hours each day besides working at Kris' Hallmark Shop near Vancouver, Washington. She is a member of Brush Prairie Conservative Baptist Church.

*Tree Tall and the Whiteskins*, her first book about Tree Tall, was published by Herald Press in 1985.